A Fine State of Affairs

Book 3

Grosset & Dunlap

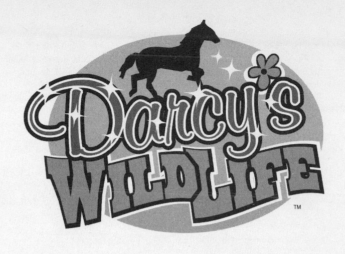

A Fine State of Affairs

Book 3

By Laura J. Burns

Based on the television series
created by Doug Tuber and Tim Maile

A Stan Rogow Book • Grosset & Dunlap

GROSSET & DUNLAP
Published by the Penguin Group
Penguin Group (USA) Inc., 375 Hudson Street, New York, New York 10014, U.S.A.
Penguin Group (Canada), 90 Eglinton Avenue East, Suite 700, Toronto, Ontario,
Canada M4P 2Y3 (a division of Pearson Penguin Canada Inc.)
Penguin Books Ltd, 80 Strand, London WC2R 0RL, England
Penguin Ireland, 25 St Stephen's Green, Dublin 2, Ireland
(a division of Penguin Books Ltd)
Penguin Group (Australia), 250 Camberwell Road, Camberwell, Victoria 3124, Australia
(a division of Pearson Australia Group Pty Ltd)
Penguin Books India Pvt Ltd, 11 Community Centre, Panchsheel Park,
New Delhi - 110 017, India
Penguin Group (NZ), Cnr Airborne and Rosedale Roads, Albany, Auckland 1310,
New Zealand (a division of Pearson New Zealand Ltd)
Penguin Books (South Africa) (Pty) Ltd, 24 Sturdee Avenue, Rosebank, Johannesburg
2196, South Africa

Penguin Books Ltd, Registered Offices:
80 Strand, London WC2R 0RL, England

Published by Grosset & Dunlap, a division of Penguin Young Readers Group,
345 Hudson Street, New York, New York 10014.
GROSSET & DUNLAP is a trademark of Penguin Group (USA) Inc.
Printed in the U.S.A.

Library of Congress Control Number: 2005021686

ISBN 0-448-44260-4   10 9 8 7 6 5 4 3 2 1

Hi again!

I'm Sara Paxton—otherwise known as Darcy Fields on <u>Darcy's Wild Life</u>. Right now, you're holding one of two brand-new books in our <u>Darcy</u> series! And if you've noticed that we're doing things a little differently this time around, it's because we're creating new and totally original stories.

Now we can take Darcy places that the T.V. show might not be able to, opening doors for lots of new and exciting experiences. We can send Darcy on a dream vacation or bring in friends from her life back in L.A.! This time, we're sending her on a camping adventure, and we're bringing the state fair (and a cute new boy!) to Bailey. Sounds exciting, right?

So, by the time you read this book, the second season of <u>Darcy</u> will be airing. And if you're a fan of the show, you can see how much my character has been growing. Darcy was shell-shocked when her mom up and moved her to Bailey, but before long, she started getting used to the simpler life. Now, Darcy has completely bonded with her new friends (both human and animal), and she's learning so much—and loving every minute of it.

Darcy's changing a lot, too, and she's trying new things all the time. It seems like there is always an adventure just around the corner, and there are so many new and exotic animals to meet . . . Life just keeps getting wilder for Darcy, and I'm so excited to be along for the ride!

Well, I hope you're enjoying the show, and I really hope you love these books! Thanks for joining me, and happy reading!

Best
Wishes!
♡ always,
Sara Paxton

Chapter 1

Clang! Crash!

"Oh, man."

Eli's voice drifted in from the kitchen. Darcy Fields shot a smile at her mother, Victoria, who sat across the dining-room table. "Looks like our breakfast is going to be late again," Victoria said in her oh-so-charming British accent.

Darcy nodded. It was just another typical morning in Bailey. Eli was dropping things, a rooster sat perched on the windowsill, and Darcy and her former-movie-star mom were hanging out far, *far* from the red carpet in Hollywood. "Kinda makes you miss brunch at the Ivy, huh?" Darcy asked.

"Not at all. *They* never had live theater." Victoria nodded toward the kitchen doorway, where Eli, the teen she'd hired to help out around the ranch, was engaged in a dish-towel tug-of-war with a goat.

Darcy sighed. She'd pretty much given up on ever convincing her mother to move back to Malibu, where movie stars—and their daughters—belonged. But you can't blame a girl for trying!

"Good morning, Fields women!" a voice called from the open window. Darcy looked over to see Brett Brennan and his brother, Brandon, peering in at them. Both wore their usual uniform of plaid shirts over jeans. Brett had on a "Toucans Can!" baseball cap, and Brandon held a . . . well, a small furry creature in his arms.

"Come in, come in!" Victoria cried. "What is that adorable thing?"

The brothers came through the door. "It's a sugar glider," Brandon said. "Don't you want to pet it?"

Darcy checked out the tiny gray creature. It had a black stripe that started at its nose and went all the way down its back to its long tail. The long fingers of its hands clung to Brandon's arm while it stared at Darcy with big brown eyes.

"Kinda," Darcy said, reaching forward. "Does it bite?"

"Only if you're made of cat food!" Brett joked. "That's what this little bugger eats."

Darcy stroked the soft fur. "Cute," she said.

"Do you want to pet him?" Brandon asked Victoria. "We're trying out animals for our petting zoo."

"You're opening a petting zoo?" Darcy asked. "With goats and ponies and stuff?"

"We're thinking more like meerkats and ocelots," Brett said.

"*Tame* ocelots," Brandon put in.

"And all the money we make from the petting zoo will go to our favorite llama rescue organization," Brett said. "After all, we can't be the *only* ones rehabilitating exotic animals."

"Well, that sounds absolutely wonderful," Victoria said. "We'll be your first customers when you open."

"But you haven't heard the best part," Brandon said. "The petting zoo is going to be at the state fair!"

Darcy waited for more info. But the Brennan brothers just stood there with big goofy grins on their faces. "Um . . . wow?" Darcy said.

"You're not kidding," Brett agreed. "We've never had a booth at the fair before!"

"Why not?" Victoria asked. "With your collection of exotic animals, I'd think you would be a big hit."

"The state fair moves around a lot," Brandon explained. "It's in a different town every year."

"We've never been close enough to get all the animals there safely," Brett said.

"But this year the fair will be in Holbrook—just one town away!" Brandon was so thrilled, he actually bounced up and down a little with the sugar glider in his arms.

"Holy cow!" Eli cried, appearing in the doorway with a gallon of milk in his hand. The goat was chewing on Eli's T-shirt, but he didn't seem to notice. "Did you just say the state fair is in Holbrook?"

"You bet," Brett said. "It'll be there for an entire week."

"All right!" Eli threw his arms in the air and jumped up and down in excitement. Unfortunately, the milk container was open—so every time Eli jumped, milk sloshed from the top. Soon enough, Eli, the goat, and the floor were covered in milk! "Aw, man," Eli said. He raced back into the kitchen for a mop.

Darcy bit her lip to keep from laughing. Poor Eli was such a klutz. But she'd never seen him so excited before. "What's the big deal about this state-fair thingie?" she asked the Brennan brothers.

"The big deal?" Brett cried. "Why, it's the best time of the whole year! It's like a huge, weeklong party."

Darcy's blue eyes sparkled. "Really?" she cried. "With ice sculptures and a raw bar and couture evening gowns?"

The Brennan brothers exchanged a confused look. "Not exactly. But there are pie-eating contests and booth games and livestock auctions," Brandon said cheerfully.

Huh. That didn't sound very glam. But maybe she just didn't understand. What kind of party had livestock at it? "Once, my friend Marina had a party at the Beverly Hilton to raise money for poodle rescue," Darcy said. "She had a bunch of poodles all dressed up in fancy costumes. Is it like that?"

The Brennan brothers laughed. "Not at all," Brett said.

"I think it sounds charming," Victoria said. "A real country fair. Are there competitions for the best produce? I've got a gigantic squash in the garden. Darcy thinks it looks like the Wicked Witch."

"It does," Darcy cried. "It's all warty and gross."

"Sounds like a winner to me," Brandon said. "You could enter it in the biggest squash competition or the ugliest squash competition—"

"Or the most creative squash competition," Brett put in.

"Also, there's a dance," Brandon said. "That's always a big deal to you kids."

"I hear they're bringing in a caller all the way from Denver," Brett said.

"A caller?" Darcy repeated. "What's that?"

"You know, to call the square dances," Brandon told her. "Should be a rockin' good time!"

"Sounds good to me," Darcy said, shrugging. Animals and vegetables and a square dance were a change of pace from the glitter of Los Angeles, but hey, a party was a party, right? And things in Bailey usually managed to surprise her and bring on more fun than she was expecting. She raised her glass of orange juice. "Here's to my first state fair!"

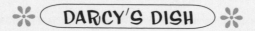

DARCY'S DISH

Hey, everyone! There's big news in Bailey this week—the state fair. What's a state fair, you ask? Well, you got me! It sounds like some kind of farming show. Or maybe an animal show. Or maybe both. One thing's for sure, though—it's definitely going to be a big change from the Cannes Film Festival. I heard that there's some kind of dance. And rides. And games. So I'm sure it'll be okay. I bet it'll even be fun! Stranger things have happened. I'll keep you posted.

"Hellllloooo!" Darcy called as she pushed open the swinging doors of Creature Comforts. "I'm five minutes early for work! I think it's a record." She wanted to be sure her friend Lindsay Adams knew about this incredible feat of earliness. Lindsay was totally serious and hardworking all the time, and she tended to think that Darcy didn't care as much about things like punctuality. But it wasn't that Darcy didn't care—it was just that things had a way of happening whenever she was on her way to work. It was hardly ever her fault when she was late. Still, it happened a lot. So being early to her shift at the veterinarian's office was a move that would get complete Lindsay approval.

If only Lindsay were there.

"Hi, Darcy," said Kevin, Lindsay's father. He was the vet here, while Lindsay mostly ran the place—keeping track of stock, helping customers, filling orders. But today Kevin was manning the counter, a pencil stuck behind his ear and a long order form laid out in front of him. "I'm glad you're here. Do you know where we keep the hypoallergenic rabbit shampoo?"

"Sure." Darcy went into the back room and grabbed a bottle from the bath supplies cabinet. Lindsay would approve of that, too. When she started working here, Darcy hadn't known anything about a vet's office. And now she had it all totally down. But was Lindsay here to see? Nope. "What are you doing?" she asked as she handed the shampoo to Kevin.

"Mrs. Park sent in her biannual list of pet supplies. I'm trying to get everything together so I can deliver it to her farm this afternoon."

"Where's Lindsay?" Darcy asked. "Doesn't she usually do that stuff?"

"Yup. But I gave her the afternoon off," Kevin said.

Darcy stared at him. The words "Lindsay" and "time off" didn't compute. Lindsay even worked on weekends. "And she took it?"

"Well, she had something very important to do," Kevin said. He narrowed his eyes at Darcy. "In fact, I'm surprised that you're here. I assumed that you'd be helping her."

"Helping her do what?" Darcy asked. Now she was starting to get suspicious. What kind of superimportant project did Lindsay have, and why hadn't she told Darcy about it?

"Tell you what. You go over to our house to see Lindsay and find out," Kevin said. "I can manage without you two for one afternoon."

"Okay," Darcy said. "Thanks."

She hurried over to where Lindsay lived with her dad and her little brother, Jack. She heard giggling coming from Lindsay's room. This day was getting weirder and weirder—Lindsay wasn't usually much of a giggler.

14

"What's going on?" Darcy demanded, pushing open the door.

Lindsay looked back at her, her pale face turning bright red. Their other friend Kathi sat on the bed. "We're trying on clothes!" Kathi said cheerfully.

Darcy stared at Lindsay in shock. Lindsay didn't try on clothes. Lindsay didn't even care whether her top matched her jeans half the time. She thought fashion was a waste of time.

So why was she wearing . . . a *dress*?

"I have to sit down," Darcy gasped. She threw herself onto the bed next to Kathi. "I think I've fallen into the Twilight Zone."

"It's no big deal," Lindsay muttered. Her cheeks were still flushed and she pulled at the skirt of the cute floral sundress she had on.

"Are you kidding?" Darcy cried. "You're not wearing denim. It's a *huge* deal! What's the story?"

"It's for the dance," Kathi said. "Isn't it great? It doesn't fit me anymore, but Lindsay's so skinny, I knew she could wear it! And I brought over a necklace and sandals and everything! Only the sandals are too big. But we can go shopping and get Lindsay her own sandals to go with it." Kathi grinned her usual big happy grin. Whenever she wasn't talking, she was smiling.

"Uh . . . it is great," Darcy said. "It looks terrific on you, Lindsay. But . . . but . . ."

"It's for the dance," Lindsay said. "At the state fair. I have to have the perfect outfit."

Speechless. Darcy was speechless. The perfect outfit was something *she* cared about. It was something *Kathi* cared about. It was even something that Darcy's *mom* cared about. But Lindsay? Lindsay only cared that her outfit was comfortable and neat. Not perfect, or fashionable, or even just plain cute. Lindsay thought that worrying about clothes was a waste of time because there were usually more important things to worry about.

"Okay, fine, so it *is* a big deal," Lindsay said, embarrassed. "People come from all over and the dance goes until after midnight . . ."

"It's basically the coolest, awesomest, most fun night of the whole entire summer!" Kathi cried. "All the boys put on ties and stuff. And there's food and punch and music and—"

"It's like a school dance, only way bigger," Lindsay cut in. "Even I know that you can't wear jeans and a T-shirt to a big dance."

"Wow," Darcy said slowly. "I guess this state fair really *is* the hugest thing to hit Bailey all year."

Chapter 2

Wild Wisdom . . . *The kinkajou lives in Central and South America and is closely related to the raccoon. It uses its tail to grasp branches as it climbs trees.*

❋ ⟨ DARCY'S DISH ⟩ ❋

What's up? It's Monday morning, and you know what that means—today is the first day of the state fair! I can't wait to see what all the buzz is about. If you ask Lindsay—or Kathi or Jack or Eli—it should be the coolest thing since sliced bread. Not that sliced bread is all that, but you know what I mean. The uncoolest thing is that I actually have to work at the fair. Creature Comforts has a booth there, offering free checkups and vaccines to whatever animals people bring in. Which is pretty decent of Kevin, you know? Those shots can be expensive! And it will be fun to check out what kinds of pets people bring in from all over the state. In fact, I better dash, or I'm gonna be late!

❋   ❋   ❋   ❋   ❋   ❋

Darcy ran out the front door, grabbing a big floppy hat on the way. She wasn't sure if the Creature Comforts booth was going to have a roof or not, and sitting all day in the sun would not be a happy situation.

"Hey, Mom!" Darcy called.

Victoria looked up and shaded her eyes. She was kneeling in some dirt that Eli had just turned over with a hoe. Darcy knew they were planting a new vegetable garden this morning. Victoria was so happy with the results of the last garden—like the giant, scary squash—that she'd decided to make a new one out in front of the house, where there was more land. This garden would be twice as big as the current vegetable garden, which apparently was a great thing. Darcy didn't see what the big deal was—did anybody really *want* twice as many vegetables? But Victoria and Eli were superexcited. They seemed to have an assembly line going—with Eli breaking ground and Victoria planting the baby plants.

"Good morning, darling!" Victoria called.

"Are the Brennan brothers here yet?" Darcy asked.

"Haven't seen them," Victoria called back.

"Hey, Darce!" Eli let go of the hoe to wave hello. The hoe fell, its handle heading straight for Victoria's head! Eli grabbed for it but missed. He jumped forward to block Victoria and accidentally stepped on the bottom of the hoe. The handle came flying back up and smashed him right in the face.

Darcy winced. "Um, hi, Eli," she replied. "Are you okay?"

"Mmpfff. Mmpftt," Eli said, holding his nose.

"Let's go get some ice for that," Victoria said, leading him inside.

Just then the Brennan brothers pulled up in their humongous pickup truck. "Ready to go, Darcy?" Brett called from the passenger side.

Darcy squinted at the truck. The flatbed was big, but the cab was pretty small. In fact, with Brett and Brandon inside, there didn't seem to be any leftover space. Darcy got a sinking feeling in her stomach. She'd been psyched when they offered to give her a ride to the fair. But maybe she should have insisted that her mom take her instead.

"Where am I supposed to sit?" she asked. "Are you guys gonna scoot over?"

Brandon laughed. "We can't do that. We'd crush the sugar gliders!" He lifted a little carrying cage from the seat between them. Two of the gray creatures stared out at Darcy.

"We made a place for you in the back," Brett said. "Between the turkey vulture and the kinkajou."

"Oh. Thanks." Darcy went around to the bed of the

pickup and stared at all the animal crates. There had to be at least ten of them. She had no idea what a turkey vulture or a kinkajou were, so she just found an empty spot and sat down. "I knew I shouldn't have worn my Dolce & Gabbana jeans today," she told a furry creature in the cage behind her. It looked like some kind of monkey, but it had a golden mane around its face. It reached out and grabbed Darcy's braid.

"Ouch!" she cried, yanking it away. "Bad . . . thingie."

The animal didn't look sorry at all. Darcy sighed. It was going to be a long ride.

"Look out!" somebody yelled.

Darcy jumped out of the way as a guy dressed in bright purple spandex whipped by her on in-line skates.

"You're walking on the course," another guy told her, pulling her to the side.

"What course?"

"The skating course," he said. Darcy glanced around. In-line skaters came flying at her from every direction, doing spins and flips and all kinds of tricks. Next to the skating course was a temporary half-pipe that kids were skateboarding on. Beyond that, a Ferris wheel rose in the distance. Delicious food smells drifted past, and music pulsed through the air. Darcy couldn't believe how big the fair was. She'd been picturing a tiny carnival, and instead it was more like the Santa Monica Pier back in California!

Now if only she could figure out where she was going.

Darcy pulled out the map that Lindsay had drawn showing her how to find the Creature Comforts booth. Unfortunately, one of the Brennan brothers' animals—they had plenty of them—had snatched the map from her pocket in the truck and taken a big bite out of it. Darcy held the mangled paper in front of her, trying to figure out which way was up. Or down. Or sideways.

One of the little squares on the map had a label on it: "Birthing Booth." That sounded familiar. Darcy spun in a slow circle, searching until she found it—a huge tent with a wooden sign that said "Birthing Booth." She hurried over and tapped on the arm of a big guy in overalls.

"Excuse me," Darcy said. "Can you tell me where—"

"Shh!" he hissed. "Bonnie's calving. We want everything quiet so she doesn't get stressed out."

Darcy stood on tiptoe and looked over his shoulder. A cow was giving birth.

"Whoa!" she cried. "Um, I mean, it's a beautiful thing, but . . . but . . . I'm gonna go." She took off, wanting to get as far away from there as possible. She'd seen animals being born before—in fact, she'd even helped deliver a baby horse. But it wasn't exactly top on her list of things to do at a fair. And besides, she was so late! She didn't want to leave poor Lindsay with all the setup work at the booth.

In front of her was a large courtyard filled with games. Basketball, whack-a-mole, water-pistol shooting, and anything else you could imagine.

"Hey there. Can you help me?" somebody asked.

Darcy turned to see a gorgeous pair of green eyes and some killer dimples. Or rather, a boy around her age *with* the eyes and the dimples . . . and a dark buzz cut and broad shoulders and a sizzling smile. "Hi," Darcy said. "And I mean that."

He laughed. "You look like a girl who has good luck," he said.

"I used to be," Darcy told him. "And then my mother moved me to the middle of nowhere, so now I'm not so sure."

"Well, can you give it a try for me?" Dimples asked. He held up a quarter. "If I get one more quarter in the bottle, I win a free roller-coaster ride."

"Cool," Darcy said. "How can I help?"

"Just blow on the quarter," he said. "For good luck."

Darcy blew softly onto the coin in his hand. She felt a blush creeping up her neck as he watched her. He was seriously cute. She was starting to see why Kathi and

Lindsay had been so excited about this fair.

The guy turned and gently tossed the quarter toward a tall glass bottle with a narrow opening at the top. It landed right on the edge . . . wavered . . . and then dropped inside.

"All right!" Dimples cried, throwing his arms in the air.

"Wow. That was a great toss," Darcy said.

"See? You're good luck." He grinned at her. "But I have to tell you, you look kinda lost."

"I am," Darcy admitted. "I'm looking for the Creature Comforts booth. My map got ruined." She handed him the piece of paper. He studied it for a few seconds.

"Well, we're in the game center. And the birthing booth is that way. And the food court is up here." He turned the map around. "And the main music stage is over there . . . so you want to go straight up this aisle and then make a left and a right."

Darcy stared at him. "How do you know where everything is already?" she asked.

"Let's just say I know my way around a state fair," he said. He gave her a wink and disappeared into the crowd.

"Thank you!" Darcy yelled after him. She continued up the aisle with a huge smile on her face. All her friends had been totally right. This fair was a *scene*!

Chapter 3

Wild Wisdom . . . *The marmoset is a small, squirrel-like monkey. Marmosets scurry through trees and communicate by chattering in shrill voices.*

By the time Darcy arrived at the Creature Comforts booth, it was almost all set up. Kevin, Lindsay, and Jack had created a mini version of the vet's office in Bailey, with a section for reception, a counter full of pet supplies for sale, and a separate back room where the animals would go for their free checkups or vaccines. The only thing missing was the old guy who always slept in the Creature Comforts waiting room.

"Sorry I'm late," Darcy said. "A critter ate my map."

"If I had a dime for every time I heard *that* excuse," Kevin joked.

"What do you need me to do?" Darcy asked, peering around the large booth.

"Uh, nothing," Jack said in his usual semisarcastic tone. His bushy brown hair swung as he shook his head at Darcy. "I was forced to do all your work for you."

Darcy winced. "Sorry."

"Take me with you next time you visit Hollywood, and we'll call it even," Jack told her.

Lindsay rolled her eyes. Her little brother was obsessed with Hollywood—even more than Darcy was! "Listen, Darce, I worked out a schedule for us this week," Lindsay said. "One of us should be at the reception desk at all times. I figure we can work together the same way we usually do, and at lunch-time we'll take turns."

"That means we can't have lunch together," Darcy pointed out.

"I know. But I think we'll survive," Lindsay said. "There's plenty to do at the fair even if you're not with your friends."

Darcy thought of the cute guy with the dimples. "I guess you're right," she said. "So do you want to go get lunch now? I was really late, so I don't mind taking the first shift here."

Lindsay looked around the booth, biting her lip. "Maybe I should show you where everything is first," she said, worried.

"Everything is exactly where it is in the office in Bailey," Jack said. "Even Darcy can figure that out."

"Thanks," Darcy said. "I think."

"Whatever," Jack replied. "I'm bored with this work talk. We're in a fair just bursting with entertainment possibilities. I'm gonna go discover the next Hilary Duff! Or maybe the next Lassie . . ." He wandered off into the crowds of people passing by.

"We're not charging for medical care, but the supplies are still for sale," Lindsay told Darcy. "We're going to keep the money in this strongbox." She showed Darcy a sturdy gray metal box. "I have the key on a chain around my neck—"

"Good," Darcy interrupted, reaching for the long chain. She pulled it up and over Lindsay's strawberry blond hair. "Now go get lunch."

"But—"

"I got it." Darcy slipped the chain over her own head. "Shoo! Go have fun!"

Lindsay still looked worried, so Darcy gave her a gentle push out into the aisle. Poor Lindsay seriously needed a coach to help her have fun. Darcy shuddered to think what Lindsay's life must've been like before Darcy moved to Bailey! Although the way Lindsay had been acting the other day—trying on a dress and talking about a dance—was enough to make Darcy think there was hope for her yet!

"Hi, I'm here for the free vaccinations," a woman

said. Darcy turned to her, all business. Well, until she saw the tiny puppy in the woman's arms.

"Hey, you wittle cutie-wootie," Darcy cooed, scratching the baby's furry yellow head.

"He needs his second round of puppy shots. Do you do that?" the woman asked.

"We sure do," Kevin replied, coming out from the examination area. "You want to help me with this, Darcy?"

"You bet!" Darcy had been giving shots to animals since her very first week on the job. She took the puppy in her arms and followed him into the back. This running-the-booth thing was going to be fun!

"That must be a really good book."

Lindsay jumped when she heard the voice right next to her ear. She lowered her book and looked up— into the big eyes of a cute boy. Immediately, she felt herself blush. "Yeah," she said, embarrassed. "It is."

She glanced back down at the book, but the words swam in front of her eyes. She was totally distracted. Boys never talked to her! Was he still there? Was she supposed to keep talking to him?

She snuck a look back up. The boy grinned and sat down at the little folding food-court table. He was eating an apple.

"What's your name?" he asked.

"Lindsay," she said. Her voice came out high and squeaky. But she couldn't help it—he was seriously gorgeous!

"I'm Carter," he said. "So you'd rather read than explore the fair, huh?"

"No," Lindsay said. "Not entirely. I just wanted to finish this chapter. I was reading it this morning, and it was a really exciting part . . ." Her voice trailed off. She felt kind of dumb talking about books to a cute guy. That would be a big Don't on Darcy's list of How to Behave Around Cuteness. She added, "I figured I'd finish this chapter and then have the rest of my lunch break to explore."

"Do you want me to go?" he asked.

"No!" Lindsay cried. She wasn't sure exactly what she was supposed to say to him, but she definitely didn't want him to leave!

"Well, if you want to finish the chapter . . ."

Lindsay closed her book. "Nope. You're right. The state fair is only once a year, and I should have fun exploring it." There. Darcy would totally approve of that. It showed a spirit of adventure—and it was kind of an invitation. Would he take it? Butterflies began to dance in her stomach.

Carter grinned. "Good for you. Want some company?"

She smiled back. She was always self-conscious around guys, but this boy was so friendly that she was beginning to relax. "Sure," she said. "I have a feeling that this state fair is going to be my favorite one ever!"

"Ally McBite, world's biggest alligator," Jack said into his mini tape recorder. "Remember to check on whether she's got an agent or not." He stuck the recorder back into the pocket of his jeans and took another look at the humongous gator. Would she be the one to make him a famous Hollywood talent manager?

Ally McBite yawned, showing all her teeth. Some of the other kids standing near the side of the booth gasped and screamed. "Later, gator," Jack said. He headed back out in search of a star.

Instead he found the most awesome booth he'd seen yet—Elmer's Fudge. The smell of chocolate drew Jack straight up to the front of the line. A tall, thin man was just placing a tray of newly made fudge into a big glass display cabinet.

"How much for the big one that's shaped like Saturn?" Jack asked.

"One dollar fifty," the guy told him.

"Tell you what," Jack said, putting on his best wheeler-dealer voice. "You give me the Saturn fudge, and I make you famous as . . . the Fudgey Astronomer. Fudge in the shape of every planet in the solar system!"

"They're pretty much all round," the guy said. "Saturn's the only interesting one."

"Fine," Jack muttered. He pulled out a quarter. "What will this get me?"

The guy handed over a piece of typical square-shaped fudge. "Thanks," Jack mumbled as he shoved it in his mouth. He chewed as he wandered farther down the main aisle. There was a line of people outside a small booth on the corner of another aisle. The entrance was draped with scarves and a beaded curtain. A sign in the shape of a crescent moon hung from a chain over the entry.

"What's so great about this place?" Jack asked a man standing in line.

"It's the Great Martoni!" the man said. "He's a famous fortune-teller."

Jack frowned. "You mean you pay him to look in a crystal ball and tell you your future?"

"Oh, no, he's much more than that," a woman in line answered. "He reads tarot cards, and I think he's also psychic!"

"Huh." Jack looked at the long line of customers. Clearly this fortune-telling thing was a business to get into—the guy was making a fortune telling fortunes! "I think I better check out this Great Martoni."

"Come on, boy! Come on," Darcy coaxed, pulling on the leash. "You can do it, Bruiser!"

But Bruiser dug his claws into the dirt and refused to budge. This was one ferret that did not want to see the doctor. Darcy looked up at Bruiser's owner, a woman in a bright pink sweatshirt who just smiled adoringly at the little ferret.

Darcy tried pleading. "Please? Please come with me?" She tugged on the leash. Bruiser pulled the other way.

Suddenly a hand swooped under Bruiser's little belly and lifted him into the air. "I'll take him in," Lindsay said. She gave Darcy a big smile, took the leash from her, and carried the ferret into the examination area.

Darcy shrugged at Bruiser's owner. "That's why Lindsay is the professional," she said. "She always knows just what to do."

In a few seconds, Lindsay returned, still with the big smile on her face.

"I know," Darcy said. "I should've thought of picking him up. I still have a lot to learn . . ." Her voice trailed off as she realized that Lindsay was totally ignoring her, humming to herself as she straightened the jar of free dog biscuits on the counter. "Hey," Darcy said. "What's going on? Usually you'd tease me for the Bruiser incident."

"Nah. How would you know you could pick him up?" Lindsay said. "He could have bitten you."

"He could have bitten *you*," Darcy pointed out.

Lindsay thought about that for a second, then laughed. "I guess I have a sixth sense about which animals are going to be aggressive. Bruiser was just scared."

Darcy narrowed her eyes suspiciously. "What's going on with you?"

"What do you mean?"

"You're all happy and understanding and light-hearted," Darcy said. "It's not like you. You're supposed to be the serious one."

"Well, you're always telling me to lighten up," Lindsay said. "I'm taking your advice."

"Oh. Well, in that case, good for you!" Darcy joked. "Is it my turn for lunch?"

"Yup. Have a great time," Lindsay practically sang.

Darcy stepped out into the throng of fairgoers. She headed for a huge bunch of helium balloons floating above all the booths. That had to be Kathi's father's tent. Mr. Giraldi owned a car dealership in Bailey, and like everyone else in town, he had a booth at the fair. When she got to the balloons, she found Kathi sitting behind the wheel of a bright red vintage Corvette. A shiny blue antique Rolls Royce was parked next to it.

"Hey, Darce!" Kathi cried. "Come sit with me!"

Darcy climbed into the passenger seat of the Corvette. "Where did these cars come from?" she asked.

"They're my dad's babies," Kathi told her. "He loves vintage cars. He wants to have a whole collection, but so far there are only two."

"Are they for sale?" Darcy asked.

Kathi shook her head, her red pigtails flying. "Dad thinks people will stop to look at these cars, and then he can tell them all about the car dealership and drum up some business. We even brought a laptop with pictures of our whole inventory on it so customers can browse right from here," she said in a rush. "I'm supposed to make sure all the chrome is shiny on these two cars. That sounds easy, right?"

Darcy opened her mouth to answer, but Kathi just rushed right on.

"Well, it's not! Everybody wants to touch the cars. There are fingerprints everywhere!"

"Oh." Darcy couldn't see any fingerprints from where she was sitting, and nobody was rushing up to touch the cars. "How come you're just sitting here then? You look like you're modeling the car."

"I wish!" Kathi giggled. "I'm just taking a break. But you know what I'm worried about?"

"What?"

"I'm worried that I'm going to spend the entire fair polishing these two cars, and I won't get to have any fun."

"Lindsay and I have to work, too," Darcy pointed out. "I think it's only younger kids like Jack who get to just hang out all day."

"At least you two have each other to talk to," Kathi said. "I'm here all alone."

"Maybe you should enter a contest or something," Darcy suggested. "Aren't there all kinds of weird contests? That would give you something to do."

Kathi's mouth fell open and her eyes lit up. "Oh. My. Gosh. That is the best idea of all time! You're a genius! Which one should I enter?"

"Well—" Darcy started. But Kathi was on a roll.

"There's the cricket race or the duck race or the frog race!" Kathi cried. "Oh, but I don't have any of those animals. Maybe I could enter the cow-milking contest. Or the bull-riding contest!"

"You know how to ride a bull?" Darcy asked, astonished.

34

"No," Kathi admitted. "I guess I don't have enough time to learn, huh? Maybe I could build a model of a house and enter it in the 'Win Your Dream Home' competition. But I'm not very good at model-building. I built a model of town hall in third grade, and it totally fell apart before I even got it to school."

"What about Skittles?" Darcy asked. "Can't you do something with her?" Skittles was Kathi's pet pug.

"You mean like put her in the working dog competition?" Kathi asked. "Maybe. I'd have to train her to pull a cart or to herd sheep. I bet she'd be really good at herding sheep. Oh, but I don't have any sheep."

Darcy tried not to laugh at the idea of little Skittles, with her flat face and her short legs, trying to herd a bunch of sheep. She wouldn't even reach their knees! "Aren't there any non–working dog things?" she asked. "Like a . . . dog beauty contest or something?"

Kathi gasped. "Yes! There's a talent contest on Saturday before the dance. There's one for humans and one for nonhumans. Skittles definitely qualifies as nonhuman."

"I'll say," Darcy replied. "What talents does she have?"

For once, Kathi was utterly silent. Darcy leaned forward and peered into her eyes, trying to make sure she was okay. She'd never seen her friend go for so long without talking before. Finally, Kathi said, "I don't think Skittles has a talent. I'm not sure she even really knows her name."

"Huh. That could be a problem," Darcy said. "Maybe you can teach her a talent before Saturday."

Kathi nodded. "I'm going to. I can definitely do it! I'll just bring her here with me and work on training her when I'm not busy wiping off fingerprints."

"Sounds like a plan." Darcy's stomach rumbled. "I'm starved. Wanna go get lunch?" she asked.

Kathi's face fell. "Sorry, I already ate. But there are lots of cool kids here. I bet you'll make ten friends on the way to the food booths."

"I'd settle for one," Darcy said with a smile. "See you later." She climbed out of the car and followed her nose toward what had to be the food court. Barbecue scents drifted through the warm air.

"Darcy! Where are you going?"

Darcy turned to see Jack hanging around outside a cool-looking booth with lots of drapery decorated with New Agey symbols.

"I'm getting lunch. Wanna come?" Darcy asked.

"Can't. I'm busy doing research," Jack said. "This Great Martoni guy has a sweet deal."

"What's a great martoni?" Darcy asked.

"He's a fortune-teller," Jack said, dropping his

voice. "I've been hanging out near the booth all morning, listening in on his sessions with customers. By the end of the day, I'll know all his tricks. Then I can go into business for myself."

Darcy gasped. "Jack! That's private stuff. You shouldn't be eavesdropping on people's futures."

"Yeah, yeah." Jack waved her off. "I won't tell anyone."

Darcy shook her head. Jack cracked her up sometimes with his get-rich-and-or-famous schemes. She ducked around a stilt walker and passed a giant tent where pumpkins were lined up in long rows. And then she heard a familiar laugh—it was Brandon, manning the Brennan brothers' petting zoo.

"Hey," Darcy greeted him. "How's it going?"

"Can't complain," he said. "Everybody loves the marmoset."

"Well, who wouldn't love a marmoset?" Darcy asked. She had no idea what a marmoset was, but that probably didn't matter.

"We did have a little incident with two of our degus," Brett said, coming over to join them. "They got into a fight over a dried carrot."

"Scary," Darcy said.

"Not really. They're both only seven inches long," Brandon told her. "It wasn't much of a fight."

"Oh. Cool." Darcy gave them a little wave. "Have fun with the zoo!"

"Thanks," Brett called as she headed off. "Come by whenever you want."

"You can pet the critters for free!" Brandon added.

I must be taking the long way to the food court, Darcy thought as the path she was on led into an area filled with carnival rides. There was a three-story-high slide, a carousel, three roller coasters in various sizes, two spinning rides, and a Ferris wheel. Darcy was looking up at the top car on the wheel when the toe of her sandal caught on something in the walkway. She fell forward with a shriek, the ground rushing toward her face—

—until a pair of arms grabbed her and pulled her back to her feet.

"Thanks," Darcy gasped. She looked up at her rescuer. It was the boy with the dimples who had helped her find the Creature Comforts booth this morning.

"No problem, good-luck girl," he said with a grin.

Darcy's heart did a little flip-flop. He remembered her!

"Sorry about the cord," the guy said.

"Cord?" Darcy asked.

"The one you tripped over?"

Darcy glanced down at her feet, where a thick orange extension cord ran across the walkway.

"I was just about to cover it," he said, holding up a thick rubber saddle-shaped thing that she assumed was a cord cover. For the first time, she noticed that he was wearing the same red T-shirt that a lot of the other ride workers wore. It said "Moon Rides."

"Do you work here?" she asked.

He nodded. "I was setting up the bumper cars, and I needed a little extra juice. I had to run the extension cord over to the next outlet."

"I love bumper cars," Darcy said. "They're the only cars I'm allowed to drive."

"Tell me about it. I still have a year before I can get my license." He rolled his eyes.

"Me too!" Darcy smiled and held out her hand. "I'm Darcy Fields."

"Daniel Moon," he said. He took her hand and held it for a few seconds.

Darcy's heart did a little happy dance. "So . . . Moon Rides," she said, nodding at his shirt. "Daniel Moon. Any relation?"

Daniel nodded. "My dad runs the bumper cars and a few other rides. We spend all summer going from fair to fair with the rides."

"Sounds like fun," Darcy said. "I used to travel a lot, too. But now I'm pretty much stuck in Bailey. Which is actually amazingly cool, most of the time."

"Are you working at the fair this week?" Daniel asked.

"Yup. My job has a booth here, so I'll be here every day," Darcy told him. "And you know where it is, too—you helped me find it this morning."

"Good," he said, looking into her eyes. "Then I can see you again."

Darcy blushed a little. "Yeah."

Daniel gestured to the rubber cord cover he was holding. "I better get this down before somebody else trips over that cord. But I'm glad you did, Darcy."

"You are?" Darcy frowned. "Why?"

"Because it gave me a chance to meet you," Daniel said. "Officially." He gave her one last dimple-filled smile before turning away to cover the cord.

Darcy could hardly stop herself from skipping off toward the food court.

DARCY'S DISH

I am seriously starting to understand why everyone was so psyched for this state fair. Because between the cool fair and the cute boy, this week is going to be amazing!

Chapter 4

Wild Wisdom . . . *The turaco is mostly bright green and blue, and its primary feathers are a crimson color. Unlike most birds, the turaco's color comes from true pigment! This means that when dipped into water, the primary feather will dye the water red.*

"I think something is blocking it," Eli said. It was Tuesday morning, and Eli and Victoria were trying to water the new garden. But nothing came out of the hose, even though the faucet was on. Eli turned the hose around and stared into the end of it, searching for a stone or a clod of dirt that might have gotten inside to block the water stream.

"Oh, perhaps it's me," Victoria said suddenly. She'd just realized she was standing on the hose. She quickly stepped off of it and turned to Eli—just as the water came rushing out the end and straight into his face!

"Hey, Mom!" Darcy called, skipping down the steps from the porch. She kissed her mother on the cheek. "Nice 'do."

"Thank you, darling," Victoria said, patting her blond hair. She'd pulled it up into a chic updo worthy of the red carpet. "You look nice, too. What's the occasion?"

Darcy looked down at her cute sherbet-orange capris and her Stella McCartney top. "Oh, you know, just another day at the state fair," she said. *Where I just might see a certain boy named Daniel for some flirting,* she added silently.

"Hmm," Victoria said. "If you say so. How do you like our garden?"

Darcy examined the neatly planted rows of little green leaves—and spotted Eli, drenched, watering them. "It looks good," she said. "Lots of . . . sprouts?"

Victoria laughed. "I know they all look similar now, but in a little while we'll have cucumbers and summer squash and pumpkins!"

"Wow?" Darcy said uncertainly. She liked cucumbers, but ever since the Wicked Witch squash, she'd been a little suspicious of all squash. And pumpkins were obviously only meant to be carved into jack-o'-lanterns. Although the Ivy restaurant back home had made delicious pumpkin ravioli . . .

"And some fruit," Victoria continued. "Cantaloupes and watermelons. Won't it be divine?"

"Yeah, watermelons are cool," Darcy said. "Good job, Mom." Suddenly she felt something not so good happening on her ankle. Something crawly and creepy and . . . yuck! Darcy shrieked and jumped back from the garden. A greenish-yellow bug with black spots skittered off her ankle and scurried back into the veggies. "Oh, gross," Darcy groaned.

Victoria shook her head with a smile. "You'll never be a gardener if you don't get used to a few insects," she said. "They come with the territory."

"Oh, well. Guess I'll just have to be a famous actress, then!" Darcy joked. "It runs in the family, you know."

Kevin's truck pulled into the driveway.

"Aren't the Brennan brothers driving you this morning?" Victoria asked, waving at Kevin.

"Nope. I just couldn't risk another day with the petting zoo on wheels," Darcy said. "Did you know there's an animal called a turaco?"

"No. What is it?"

Darcy opened her mouth to answer, but a horn blast from Kevin's truck cut her off. "Come on, Darce! I've got to get to the fair and start earning my millions!" Jack called from the truck. He was reaching over his father to lean on the horn.

Darcy and her mom shared a smile. "Well, you can't keep the future Donald Trump waiting," Victoria said. "Have fun."

"Thanks, Mom," Darcy said, thinking of Daniel. "I will!"

"Check out that booth right across from ours," Darcy said as she and Lindsay set up the Creature Comforts booth for the day. She read the banner over the entrance. "'The Wave of the Future.' What do you think that means?"

Lindsay shrugged. "Maybe they sell fish."

"Surfboards," Jack put in from his perch on the makeshift counter. "They teach surfing. I met them yesterday."

"Surfing?" Darcy said doubtfully. "At a state fair? In the middle of the country? Where's the water?"

"They don't need water. They've got some kind of machine," Jack said

Darcy and Lindsay exchanged a look. A surfing machine? That didn't sound normal.

"Hey, Linds, can you watch the booth for a few minutes?" Darcy asked. "I have to check this out. I happen to be a great surfer, you know."

"Really?" Lindsay asked.

"Okay, I'm not *great*," Darcy said. "But I can surf. Nobody grows up in Malibu without learning basic surfing skills."

"This I have to see," Lindsay said. "It's so annoying

that we can't leave the booth at the same time."

Darcy grinned. "Ah, but we can. Jack can keep an eye on things for a few minutes. Right, Jack?"

"What's in it for me?" he asked.

"My eternal gratitude," Darcy told him.

He raised an eyebrow.

"And I'll buy you a funnel cake," she added.

"Done," Jack said.

"No way," Lindsay protested. "We can't leave. What if a customer comes?"

"If anybody shows up, Jack can just yell for us. We'll be only ten feet away," Darcy pointed out.

"Oh, don't worry. I'll yell," Jack drawled.

"Cool. Let's go." Darcy grabbed Lindsay's arm before she could protest again. She hurried her friend across the aisle and into the entrance of the Wave of the Future. It was a much smaller booth than theirs. In fact, it was really only big enough to hold a surfboard, which was lying flat on the ground.

"Customers!" cried a guy around their age. He came rushing over to them, an excited look on his face. "Hi!" He grabbed Darcy's hand and shook it enthusiastically. His long blond hair tumbled around his face.

"Uh . . . hi," Darcy replied. "I'm Darcy."

"I'm Lindsay," Lindsay said. The guy grabbed her hand and shook it, too.

"Righteous," the guy said. "I'm Michael, but everybody calls me Mikey. That's my brother, Alex."

Darcy peered around him and noticed another guy asleep on a chair at the side of the booth. "Alex!" Mikey yelled.

Alex started and jumped up. He rushed over to stand next to his brother, wearing an identical excited expression. In fact, everything about him was identical to Mikey. Same blond hair, same slightly dorky smile, same dark eyes. The only difference was that Mikey's hair was long and Alex's was supershort. "You're twins," Darcy said.

"How can you tell?" Alex asked, acting genuinely confused.

"Um . . ." Darcy had no idea how to answer him.

"Just kidding." Alex laughed.

"Don't mind him," Mikey said. "What can we do for you *chiquitas*? Are you here to learn surfing? 'Cause that would be truly bodacious."

Darcy had to laugh at his surfer-dude talk. She'd never met an actual surfer in Malibu who talked like that.

"Darcy already knows how to surf," Lindsay said. "But my brother said you had some kind of machine?" She shot a nervous glance back at the Creature Comforts booth, checking for customers.

"Oh, are you Jack's sister?" Alex cried. "The little

man with the big hair, right? He was in here yesterday."

"I'm surprised you remember him," Lindsay said.

"Well, he's got a big personality for such a little dude," Alex said with an approving nod.

"And business has been pretty slow," Mikey added. "You guys are our first customers. Besides Jack."

Darcy bit her lip. "I don't think we're really customers. We just wanted to see how you planned to teach surfing with no water."

"With our invention, the superfabulous Simu-Surf," Alex said. "Watch!"

He jumped onto the surfboard on the floor, positioning himself with his feet apart and his knees bent. When he was ready, Mikey hit a button on a remote control. All of a sudden, the surfboard came to life. It rose up on two hydraulic metal legs hidden underneath it. Then the legs pumped up and down, one at a time, lifting the board in an uneven motion.

Alex surfed on top of it.

Darcy burst out laughing. "That *does* look like surfing," she said.

"Did you guys really invent this?" Lindsay asked. She might be worried about leaving the booth, but she couldn't help being impressed.

"Yeah. We're trying to convince our mom to help us go into business," Mikey replied. "She said if we make five hundred dollars at this fair, she'll believe there's a market for it."

"Can I try?" Darcy asked. "How much does it cost?"

"Ten bucks," Alex told her. "But for our neighbor at the fair, it's free!"

"Thanks," Darcy said. "But you're never going to make money if you give out free rides."

"Lindsay! Darcy! Customer!" Jack bellowed from across the aisle.

"We have to go," Lindsay said. "Sorry."

"Bummer," Mikey replied.

"I'll come back and try the Simu-Surf another time," Darcy promised him. "And we'll tell everyone we know to come by, too."

"Sweet. Thanks!" Mikey walked out to the aisle with them. "Nice to meet you, neighbors!"

Darcy waved over her shoulder as she and Lindsay ran back to their booth.

❊ ⟨ DARCY'S DISH ⟩ ❊

You're not going to believe this: I might be able to get some surfing in, right here in the greater Bailey area! I told you this state fair had everything. A cute boy, cool rides, and now surfing! These two kids who invented the surfing simulator must be really smart. I think

they're frustrated surfer boys—trapped in the middle
of the country with no water. Is that tragic or what?
Somebody should make a movie about them. Hmm . . .
maybe I can star in it!

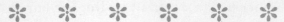

"Are you sure you don't want any more?" Carter
asked that afternoon. "There're still two curly fries
left."

Lindsay groaned and shook her head. "I'm
stuffed. You eat them."

He popped a fry into his mouth and wiggled his
eyebrows comically. She laughed, feeling her cheeks
grow warm. She felt as if she had a permanent blush
around Carter. He was so cute and sweet and funny.
She was totally crushing on him, that's what Darcy
would say. And he'd never even mentioned the fact
that she was constantly beet red and embarrassed
around him!

"I'm glad you could have lunch today, Lindsay,"
he said. "I really have fun with you."

"Me too," Lindsay replied, her heart beating faster.
"Thanks for coming to the Future Veterinarians booth
with me. I know it's kind of dorky."

"It is not," he said. "I think it's pretty amazing
that you're already planning for your future."

"I don't know if I'm *planning*," Lindsay said. "Just thinking about it. You know, getting all the info."

Carter reached across the table and took her hand, and every single thought of her future career plans flew out of her head. He was holding her hand! "I've never met anyone like you, Lindsay," he said. "You're so responsible and mature. You're a real intellectual."

"Is that good?" Lindsay asked.

"Of course it's good," he cried. "A girl with brains who's as pretty as you? You're amazing."

Lindsay grabbed the last fry, trying to cover her raging embarrassment. How could he be so perfect? Everything he said and did was exactly what she thought the perfect guy would say and do. Part of her wanted to run around shouting at the top of her lungs how much she liked him. But another part of her wanted to keep this amazing feeling all to herself.

"So how come you're always at the fair?" she asked. "Do you work here, too?"

"Yup," he said. "I run the Whip. You know, that ride where the cars swing from side to side?"

"I love that ride," Lindsay said.

"It's sort of a family business, like you with the veterinarian office," Carter told her. "But I don't know that I'm planning to run the Whip for my future!"

She smiled. "Well, I don't know for *sure* that I'm going to be a vet. Maybe I'll end up running the Whip!"

He laughed, then got serious. "Listen, Lindsay," he said, his cheeks turning as red as hers. "You know about the dance on Saturday, right?"

Lindsay nodded. The butterflies flying in her stomach felt more like giant birds.

"Do you want to go with me?" he asked. "As my date?"

A tingly feeling started at the tips of her toes and rushed all the way up through her body. He was asking her out! She'd never had a date for the state-fair dance before. She found herself just staring at him with a big grin on her face.

"Is that a yes?" he asked.

"Yes," Lindsay cried. "I would love to!"

"What time did Lindsay leave for lunch?" Darcy asked as she held a rabbit while Kevin gave it a shot.

"Every time you ask, I'm going to give you the same answer, you know," Kevin teased her. "You must be really hungry—you're so anxious for Lindsay to get back."

"Yeah. I forgot to eat breakfast," Darcy said. She felt a little guilty for lying. The truth was that she hadn't seen Daniel all day, and her only hope was to find him during lunch. On the upside, she was so distracted by thinking of cute flirty things to say to him that she didn't even mind when a llama spit at her during its exam—well, since it didn't manage to hit her.

When Darcy went out to get their next patient from the waiting area, she scanned the aisle for Lindsay. No luck. Mikey waved at her from across the way, and Alex gave a peace sign. Darcy waved back, but she couldn't muster up a smile. She wanted Lindsay to get back already! With a sigh, she took the leash of the waiting Saint Bernard and brought him in for his rabies vaccination.

"Here we go, King," Kevin said soothingly, giving the big dog a shot. He patted King on the head and checked his patient sheet. "Wait till you see the next one, Darcy," he said excitedly. "It's a boa constrictor with skin mites!"

"Skin mites?" Darcy cried, wrinkling her nose. "Wait. *Boa constrictor?*"

"Why don't you take King back to his owners and get the snake?" Kevin said. "I know I brought some ivermectin from the office. Now where did I put it?" He began searching through his bag for the skin medication.

Darcy took the dog and walked slowly back out to the waiting area. She was *not* looking forward to carrying a giant skin-challenged snake. Sure, she'd gotten somewhat used to weird animals and gross diseases while working at Creature Comforts. But that didn't mean she *always* liked them!

"Hey, Darce!" Lindsay sang when Darcy stepped into the waiting area.

"Lindsay, you're back!" Darcy cried. "I've been waiting for you."

Lindsay glanced at her watch—which wasn't her usual digital Timex, Darcy noticed. In fact, it was a cute little watch with a hot-pink leather band. "Am I late?" Lindsay asked.

"No," Darcy admitted. "I was just, um, hoping you'd be here to help me with the boa constrictor."

"His scales are all messed up. We're pretty sure it's mites," the snake's owner said. He climbed to his feet, the huge snake draped over his shoulders.

"No problem. I'll take him," Lindsay reached for the snake.

"Wait. I can help," Darcy offered. "You don't want to get snake all over your cute T-shirt." Darcy narrowed her eyes at Lindsay's Indian-print top. Since when did Lindsay wear prints?

"Oh, that's okay." Lindsay expertly took the snake and headed off into the examination room. "Have a great lunch, Darce!" she called over her shoulder.

Darcy heard her humming as she vanished behind the curtain separating the two areas. *What could be worth humming about with a snake in your arms?* Darcy wondered. But she didn't have time to stay and find out. She had to go see Daniel!

She headed straight for the rides. As soon as she got to the bumper cars, she spotted him. He was buckling a little kid into a car, his green eyes sparkling as he joked with the boy.

"Daniel, hey!" Darcy called, waving.

He glanced up and gave her one of his gorgeous smiles. She waited for him to finish strapping everyone else into the ride and turn it on. She hadn't had such a huge crush on a boy since . . . well, since ever!

"Hi, Darcy," he said, coming over to her as people began smashing their bumper cars together.

"I was wondering if you wanted to get lunch," Darcy said, keeping her voice casual. "But it looks like you're busy."

"Nah, I can take some time," Daniel said. "My dad's over at one of his other rides, but one of the other workers can cover for me here."

"Really?" Darcy asked.

"Sure." He gave her a wink and headed over to the ride entrance. A thin girl was taking tickets there. Daniel gestured toward Darcy and the girl nodded. Darcy thought she looked annoyed. *Maybe she's just jealous,* she thought. *I bet every girl who meets Daniel has a crush on him.*

"All set," Daniel said. "Let's go to the food court."

"Great. I'm starving," Darcy told him. "I'm thinking maybe some chicken satay with peanut sauce."

"Some what?" Daniel asked.

"It's kind of like an Indian shish kebab," Darcy said. "You know, with the chicken on a stick."

"Huh. I'm thinking the only thing you'll find on a stick here is a corn dog," Daniel told her. "Are you used to getting Indian food at a fair?"

"This is my first state fair, actually," Darcy said. "I guess they have them in California but not usually in Malibu. Or Beverly Hills. Or Hollywood. Or even—"

"Hold on," Daniel interrupted. "You're from Malibu?"

"Yup. Born and raised. Until my mom flipped out and moved us here," Darcy told him. "How about you? Where are you from?"

"All over," Daniel said. "Dad and I move around all summer, and then wherever we end up in the fall is where I go to school for that year."

"That sounds hard," Darcy said. Sure, she'd traveled all over the world, going on location when her mom was making movies. But home had always been Malibu. They'd never moved at all until they came to Bailey. And now home was definitely Bailey.

"I like it," Daniel said. "I get to meet all kinds of really cool people." He gave her a little nudge with his shoulder, and Darcy giggled.

When they reached the food court, Darcy headed straight for the booth she'd eaten at yesterday. They didn't have chicken satay, but they did have totally yummy grilled corn on the cob.

"No way," Daniel said, grabbing her hand. "It's corn-dog time for you."

"Wait, you were serious about that?" Darcy asked. "What is a corn dog, anyway?"

"It's a hot dog on a stick," Daniel said. "Surrounded by cornmeal."

Oh, gross, Darcy thought. "Um . . . sounds great," she said out loud. "But I think I'm gonna stick with veggies today."

"Oh, no. You've obviously never had a corn dog, and I can't let you experience your first state fair without eating a genuine corn dog." Daniel tugged on her hand, and Darcy just couldn't resist him. He was holding her hand! And he was probably kidding about the corn-dog thing—who would put cornmeal on a perfectly good frank?

But soon enough Darcy found herself standing in front of a booth with a picture of a giant yellow . . . *thing* . . . on a stick. "Am I just supposed to take your word for it that there's a hot dog in there?" she asked.

Daniel just laughed. When they got to the front of the line, he pulled out a dollar. "One corn dog, please."

"One?" Darcy asked, confused. "Aren't you having one, too?"

"Nah. I'm not really hungry," Daniel said.

The girl at the booth handed him the fried horror-on-a-stick, and he presented it to Darcy.

"Wow," Darcy said, staring at it. "Thanks."

How was she going to get out of eating this thing? Maybe she could accidentally drop it—but that would be really rude. After all, Daniel had been nice enough to buy it for her. Maybe she could distract him and then dump it in the trash while he wasn't looking. But would he really believe she'd eaten the whole thing that fast?

"Come on, dig in," he said with that gorgeous smile.

Darcy studied the thing. It was on a stick, like a Popsicle. Maybe she was supposed to lick it. She did. Daniel almost fell over laughing.

"You don't lick it! You bite it," he cried.

Darcy laughed, too. "Well, you're lucky I licked it, or I would never have eaten it! At least now I know what it tastes like."

"What does it taste like?"

"A corn muffin," Darcy said. "Like the ones from my favorite bakery on Melrose Avenue." She took a tiny bite. It tasted weird, sort of like a giant pig in a blanket—if the blanket were made of a yummy corn muffin.

"I've never met anyone like you, Darcy," Daniel told her. "You're so sophisticated."

Darcy waved her corn dog at him. She didn't feel very sophisticated, but she was totally having fun.

"Do you want to go to the dance with me on Saturday?" Daniel asked.

"Absolutely!" Darcy cried.

DARCY'S DISH

Breaking news: Corn dogs? Kind of delicious. I mean, they're not fine dining. But outside on a beautiful summer day, they taste pretty darn good. And even more breaking news: I have a date for the dance! Seriously, could this state fair get any better?

Chapter 5

Wild Wisdom . . . *Adult striped cucumber beetles prefer cucumbers, watermelons, cantaloupes, pumpkins, winter and summer squash, and gourds—but they'll also eat corn, peas, beans, and plant blossoms.*

"But I don't understand," Victoria cried into the phone on Wednesday morning. "How can there be so many of them already?" She frowned as she listened to the answer.

Darcy pulled the OJ from the fridge and glanced at her mother with concern. Victoria seemed really upset by something. Also, she was wearing muddy rubber gardening boots—with her Pucci-print silk bathrobe! Clearly, she'd been busy this morning before Darcy had even dragged herself out of bed.

Finally, Victoria hung up, shaking her head.

"What's the sitch?" Darcy asked.

"It's the beetles—they've overrun my new garden," Victoria cried. "Come see." She grabbed Darcy's hand

and pulled her to the front door. Darcy barely had time to stick her feet in her flip-flops before her mother had dragged her all the way out to the garden. "Look!" Victoria cried, her expression tragic.

Darcy looked. It all seemed normal. Then she looked closer—and screamed. Yellow bugs with black spots ran all over the place. Yesterday Darcy had seen one of them. Today she was looking at hundreds! "Oh, yuck," she cried. "What are they?"

"They're cucumber beetles," Victoria said. "Apparently they came with the vegetable plants I bought at the nursery."

Darcy wrinkled her nose. "I hope you didn't have to pay extra for them," she cracked.

"The woman at the nursery says it's highly unusual," Victoria told her. "The larvae usually pupate in soil, but she thinks these plants must've had some beetle larvae actually attached to the roots."

"Ew," Darcy said. *Larvae* and *pupate* were two words she really never needed to hear again.

"I know," Victoria agreed. "And it's truly a disaster. These beetles are very destructive."

"Are they gonna eat us?" Darcy asked, alarmed.

"No, silly, they're going to eat the plants," Victoria said. "My garden will be ruined before it's even full-grown."

Just then, Kevin's truck pulled into the driveway.
He got out, followed by Lindsay and Jack. "That's a
new look for you, Darcy," Kevin joked. "It'll be a big
hit at the fair."

Darcy glanced down at herself and realized she
was still wearing her pajamas with the little pieces of
toast printed on them. "Oh, uh . . . I'm not exactly
ready yet," she said. "I guess I slept late, and then—"

"Just look at my garden!" Victoria interrupted.
"What am I going to do?"

Kevin peered into the garden and winced. "Uh-
oh. Cucumber beetles."

"That's bad," Lindsay said sympathetically.
"They're hard to get rid of. What kinds of food are
you growing?"

"Cucumbers and squash and melons," Darcy
answered for her mother. Victoria was too busy staring
at the bugs and wringing her hands in distress.

This time, all three of the Adamses winced.
"Yikes," Lindsay said. "You've basically planted a
garden full of all their favorite foods."

Eli came riding up on his bike, pedaling furiously. "I got it!" he yelled, holding up a bottle in
one hand. Unfortunately, his other hand didn't have
control over the handlebars, and the bike veered off
the driveway and into a little ditch on the side of the

pavement. He tumbled forward and landed in the dirt. "Aw, man," Eli muttered.

"What is that?" Victoria asked as he picked himself up.

"I swung by the nursery to see if they could help with the beetles, and they gave me this." He handed the bottle to Victoria. "They said to put it on the plants now, and we might be able to save them."

Victoria studied the label on the plastic bottle. "Oh, no," she said. "I'm not using this. It's a pesticide." She looked up at Kevin. "I've decided on a strict no-pesticides policy for my ranch. They're awful chemicals! They destroy the environment."

Kevin nodded. "They can be pretty bad. But sometimes you have no choice. With a beetle infestation like this, you may have to use pesticides."

"I simply won't do it," Victoria insisted. "There must be another way."

"You can invite all your Hollywood friends over for a beetle-stamping party," Jack suggested. "I'd be glad to help you coordinate."

Darcy was happy to see her mother crack a smile. "No, Jack, I don't think that will work," Victoria said.

"Hollywood types are afraid of bugs," Darcy told him.

"Then you need to find a natural enemy," Lindsay

suggested. "Something to eat the beetles."

"What a wonderful idea," Victoria said. "What eats cucumber beetles?"

"Well . . . spiders, for a start," Kevin told her. "Spiders eat anything. But your garden is out of balance—there are too many cucumber beetles for any normal population of spiders to handle."

"Then I'll just have to add more spiders," Victoria said brightly. Then her face fell. "Um . . . where exactly do I find more spiders?" she asked.

"We'll go into the woods and hunt for them," Eli said. "Then we'll bring them back here in jars and release them into the garden."

"Marvelous," Victoria said.

"See if you can find wolf spiders," Kevin suggested. "They're excellent hunters, and they love cucumber beetles."

"That's perfect," Victoria replied. "Wolf spiders. They sound so rugged and wild!"

"Yeah. They're big and hairy with thick, stout bodies and eight eyes," Kevin said happily.

"Oh." Victoria looked less than thrilled about that. "Wonderful."

Darcy began to squirm around. She felt as if she had to scratch her legs. And her arms. Oh, and her face, her back, and her stomach. "Can we please stop talking about bugs?" she begged. "I'm starting to feel all . . . crawly."

"You have to go inside and change anyway," Lindsay pointed out. "You don't want us to be late to the fair, do you?"

Late to the fair meant late to see Daniel. "No way," Darcy cried. "I'll be out in ten seconds!" She charged toward the house. She couldn't wait to get to the fair!

"I'm bored," Darcy complained to Kathi. "It's been so slow today! Don't people need checkups for their pets on Wednesdays?"

"I dunno," Kathi said. "There was hardly anyone at my dad's tent this morning, either." She had Skittles with her and was holding out a dog biscuit over the pug's head. "Up!" she commanded. "Skittles, up!"

Skittles just licked her chops and whined.

"Oh, all right," Kathi said, handing over the biscuit.

"Maybe that's why she won't do anything," Darcy commented. "You give her treats for just sitting there and ignoring you."

"I know, but she's so cute!" Kathi picked up the little dog and showered kisses all over her wrinkly head. "I can't resist her."

"What talent are you trying to teach her?" Darcy asked.

"I was thinking I'd teach her to walk on her hind legs. And then I'll put a tutu on her and say that she's a ballet dancer," Kathi said. "Wouldn't that be so funny?"

Darcy studied Skittles's flat face and her muscular body. She would be the ugliest ballet dancer in history. "That would be pretty funny," she admitted.

Kathi put the dog down, grabbed another biscuit, and tried again.

Darcy sighed. "I wish I could go out and explore the fair. I haven't even checked out the textile tent yet. My mom said that would be the place to get interesting fabric for scarves and stuff."

"Yeah. Last year, I got a bolt of this cool tie-dyed cotton, and I used it as a bedspread, well, at least until I spilled grape juice on it. It totally stained!" Kathi bounced up and down as she talked. When she was finished, she blew a big bubble with her gum. Skittles barked.

"I wonder where Lindsay is," Darcy said. "She was supposed to be back from lunch ten minutes ago."

"Maybe she figured she could take extra time since it's so slow today," Kathi said.

"Lindsay? No way," Darcy said. "You know her, she's always on time. It's, like, encoded in her DNA or something. She thinks it's irresponsible to be late."

"That's true," Kathi said. "I don't think Lindsay's ever been late for anything since I've known her."

"It's what makes us so perfect as friends," Darcy said. "She's always on time; I'm never on time. She's all work; I'm all play. She's serious; I'm fun. We balance each other out. We're like yin and yang."

"You're not all play," Kathi said. "If you were, you wouldn't be here at the booth even though there are no customers. You'd be off, you know, playing."

"It's true. Lindsay has been a good influence on me," Darcy said.

"So maybe you've been a good influence on her," Kathi suggested. "Maybe she's off having fun."

"Hmmpf," Darcy said. Usually she'd be psyched at the idea of Lindsay being a little irresponsible and having some fun. But today all it meant was that she had to wait even longer to go see Daniel. She'd been hoping that they would have time to get lunch and then explore the fair together.

"Skittles, up!" Kathi begged. Skittles lay down and yawned.

"Can I try?" a voice called.

Darcy glanced over toward the Wave of the Future booth to see Mikey watching them. He looked bored. "Come on over," Darcy called.

He headed across the aisle and gave her a grin. "Business is slow today, huh?"

"Even for you guys?" Darcy asked.

"Yeah. Yesterday we had one customer. Today? None," he said. "It's truly wretched, dude."

"Today is Contest Day," Kathi explained. "Everybody is over at the playing fields. They set up all the tables with the pies and the food for judging. And then there are rows and rows of giant pumpkins and squashes and watermelons and stuff. And then there are, you know, frog races and duck races and snail races. It's a total crowd-pleaser. Nobody comes to the booths on Contest Day."

"Wow. I wish I could be there instead of here," Darcy said. "I've never seen a snail race."

"Nah. Then you wouldn't be here hanging with us," Mikey said with a grin. "What do you want the dog to do?" he asked Kathi.

"I'm trying to get her to walk on her hind legs," Kathi said. "You know, like a ballet dancer. But so far she won't even *stand* on them, let alone walk on them."

Mikey took a dog biscuit from the biscuit-shaped bowl on the counter and held it up over Skittles's head.

"Skittles, *up*!" he said in a deep, commanding voice. Skittles's brown eyes widened, and she stuck her two front paws up in the air.

Even Darcy sat up a little straighter.

"Good dog," Mikey said in his normal voice, feeding her the biscuit.

"Wow," Darcy said. "You were really commanding."

"Yeah, you have to, like, use a strong voice so she knows you're the alpha dog," Mikey said.

"Alpha dog?" Kathi asked.

"Top dog. The one in charge. The big Kahuna," Mikey explained.

"How do you know so much about training dogs?" Darcy asked.

"Alex and I used to breed poodles," he told her. "We'd train them for dog shows. That was our last business, before we discovered surfing."

"You've had *two* businesses already?" Darcy asked. "Wow. I feel like such a slacker."

"Nah. Nobody wanted to buy the poodles, either," Mikey said. "We didn't make any money."

"What about all the dogs?" Kathi asked.

"We have six pet poodles," he replied. "They're awesome!"

"Mikey, someone's at your booth," Darcy hissed. "He looks totally promising!" *Where did that lingo come from?* she wondered, hearing her own words.

Mikey spun around and stared at the long-haired teenage guy who stood studying the Wave of the Future sign. "Dudes, I gotta bolt," he said. He scrambled over to his booth and started chatting up the surfer wannabe.

"Skittles, up!" Kathi bellowed in as deep a voice as she could muster.

Skittles lifted her front paws in the air and tried to balance on her back paws. But her chest was so muscular and heavy and her back legs were so scrawny that she slowly fell over sideways before she ever managed to stand.

Darcy giggled. "I think that may be the best she can do," she said.

"Are you sure you have to go back to work already?" Lindsay asked. She and Carter were having such a great time that she didn't want to say good-bye even though she was late getting back to the booth. She knew Darcy would want to know why. She didn't really want to tell her friend about Carter yet—as much as she liked him, she still couldn't even think about him without getting superembarrassed. She couldn't imagine actually *talking* about him. What if Darcy teased her? But spending more time with Carter was totally worth it. "You know, everybody's at the playing fields watching the contests," she added. "There's probably not a single person waiting for the Whip."

"My father will be mad if he knows I've been goofing around all day," Carter replied. "Besides, aren't you tired of the roller coaster?"

"We've only gone on it four times," Lindsay joked. Carter had all kinds of free roller-coaster tickets, and when he'd heard it was her favorite ride, he'd taken her on it—over and over. There was no line. Once, they'd been the only people on the whole ride!

"I have time for one more thing," Carter said. "How about a game?"

"I'm not very good at games," Lindsay admitted. "That's more my brother's thing."

"Then I'll play." He led her over to a booth with a basketball hoop on the wall inside. "I'll win you something. What do you want?"

Lindsay's heart did a happy little flip-flop. He was the perfect date! "Um . . . how about one of the stuffed animals?" she said. "A cat?"

The guy at the booth whistled. "She's got expensive

taste," he teased. "That cat is the hardest one to win."

"Oh, then never mind," Lindsay said quickly, embarrassed. She was so bad at this dating thing! Maybe she should have asked for a small animal, like the turtle or something. The truth was, she wasn't really into stuffed animals. But it was incredibly sweet that Carter wanted to win one for her. She didn't want to disappoint him. "I don't need the cat."

"No sweat. I can do it," Carter told her. He paid the guy, picked up a basketball, and shot. He got three out of five baskets.

"That will win you a free cotton candy," the guy at the booth said.

"That's good. I'll take that," Lindsay told Carter.

"No way," he said. "I'm getting you the cat." He paid for another turn. This time he got only two out of five baskets.

Lindsay bit her lip. She felt really bad for saying she wanted the cat. Poor Carter was doing his best, but it was a hard game to win. "I really don't need the stuffed cat," she told him, taking his hand.

"Yes, you do," he replied. He squeezed her hand. "Third time is the charm." He took another turn— and made all five baskets.

"Nice," the guy at the booth said. "The stuffed cat

it is." He reached up and pulled one of the big pink cats off the hook where it hung. Carter handed it to Lindsay.

She grinned at him. Feeling bold, she leaned forward and gave him a kiss on the cheek, her heart slamming against her rib cage.

"See?" Carter said to the guy at the booth. "It was worth it!"

"So then he asked me to the dance," Darcy said. "He's such a sweetie!"

"I can't believe you have a date," Kathi replied excitedly. "I've never had a date for the dance before! But you'll still hang out with me, right? You'll still come to the talent show first?"

"Of course," Darcy assured her. "I wouldn't miss Skittles's big debut." She hadn't meant to tell her friends about Daniel yet. She'd kind of wanted to keep him to herself a little longer. But with the fair so slow today and Kathi hanging out at the booth, it had just sort of popped out. And Kathi was totally into boys. Lindsay would probably just roll her eyes if Darcy told her about Daniel. It wasn't that Lindsay didn't like boys. She just thought crushes were a waste of time.

"Hello, ladies," Jack drawled, ambling up to the Creature Comforts booth.

Jack's shaggy brown hair was covered by a tall purple-and-gold turban, and he wore a long purple robe over his jeans. "I'd like you to meet the Great Jacktoni!" He bowed, and his turban fell off.

Darcy raised her eyebrows at Kathi.

"Guess I better strike the bowing part," Jack muttered, picking up the headpiece and slapping it back on. "Anyway, don't ya like the name? Catchy, huh?"

"The Great Jacktoni," Darcy said. "What does it mean?"

"Nothing," Jack told her. "It's just my stage name. Or rather, my fortune-telling name." He began wandering around the empty waiting area of the booth, looking around as if sizing it up.

"What are you doing?" Kathi asked.

"I'm trying to find the perfect locale for my mystical headquarters," Jack said. "I think this corner will do." He grabbed two of the folding chairs from the waiting area and set them up facing each other in one corner. Then he glanced around, spotted a spare crate for a dog, and pulled it over until it was sitting between the two chairs. He pulled an old sheet from his backpack and draped it over the crate.

"Hey! What if we need that crate to keep a patient in?" Darcy asked.

"I don't see any patients," Jack pointed out.

"Well . . . it could happen," Darcy said.

"I still don't get it," Kathi said. "What are you going to do?"

"I'm gonna tell fortunes," Jack said. "And make tons of money doing it!"

"But Jack, you're not psychic," Darcy said. "How are you going to tell people's futures?"

"No problem," he said, waving her off. "I've been watching the Great Martoni for two days now. I know all his tricks."

"Ooh, I went to him last year!" Kathi cried. "It was spooky—he told me my favorite teacher was going to get married and she did, and then he said my father would sell three trucks in a row and he did. And then he said I'd meet a star, which I totally did when I met your mom, Darce!" She sucked in a breath and kept on going. "He did a tarot card reading, and I asked the cards whether I would get my own cell phone and the cards said I would, and then I told my dad, and he said—"

"Right, it's all about the cards," Jack interrupted. "I watched Martoni. All you have to do is shuffle the cards, make the person pick seven of them, and then you look at the cards all thoughtful and stuff. And then you tell the person all kinds of good stuff and say it's going to happen."

"Jack!" Darcy cried. "That's not how you read tarot cards."

"Sure it is," he said. He pulled a handmade sign from his backpack and taped it onto the back of one of the chairs. It said "The Great Jacktoni: Fortunes told $5."

"Five dollars?" Kathi said. "That's pretty expensive."

"I'm worth it," Jack replied confidently.

"Sorry I'm late!" Lindsay called, rushing into the booth, her cheeks flushed. She quickly shoved her new stuffed cat behind the counter before anyone could notice. Then she glanced at Jack's fortune-telling station. "What's going on?"

"Your brother's crazy," Darcy told her.

"Well, I know *that*," Lindsay said. She reached out and flicked Jack's turban so that it fell over his eyes.

Darcy looked her friend up and down. Lindsay was dressed in a really cute pair of cropped jeans with embroidery on the cuffs. Her hair hung loose around her face, even though she almost always wore it in a sensible ponytail. And around her wrist was not one but two bracelets.

Plus, Lindsay had that same goofy smile she'd been wearing all week.

"Why were you so late getting back?" Darcy asked.

"I just lost track of time," Lindsay said, not meeting her eyes. "Why don't you take an extra-long lunch, too? You know, to make up for it."

"Okay!" Darcy chirped. She grabbed her purse. She wasn't going to wait around until Lindsay changed her mind about that one.

"I'd better get back to my booth, too," Kathi said. "My dad will be having a conniption about finger-prints on the chrome." She looked down at Skittles. "Skittles, *come!*" she said commandingly. Skittles immediately got up and followed her.

"Righteous!" Mikey called from across the aisle, giving her a thumbs-up.

"Hey, did that guy take a surfing lesson on the Simu-Surf?" Darcy asked him.

"Negative," Mikey said. "He didn't have any cash with him. But he said he'd come back."

Darcy smiled. "I'm sure he will." She gave him a little wave and hurried off to find Daniel. She went straight to the bumper cars. Daniel's dad let him oversee the bumper cars most of the time. And sure enough, there he was, working the switch that turned the ride on and off.

"Hi, Darcy," he said. "I was wondering if I'd see you today. I thought you might be over at the contests."

"Nope, I'm just working. Sorry it's so late," Darcy said. "Do you want to go get lunch with me?"

Daniel winced. "I can't. My father wants me to help him oil the gears on one of his other rides sometime soon. He might call for me any minute."

"Oh." Darcy's heart sank. She'd been waiting all day to see him, and now he had no time?

"Tell you what, though," Daniel said. "Why don't you hang out here with me for a little while?"

"Aren't you busy running the ride?" Darcy asked.

"No, I can get somebody else to do it. In fact, I wouldn't mind going on the bumper cars myself. How about you?" Daniel grinned at her.

"Are you kidding? I'd love to!" Darcy said. "Let's go."

Daniel called a guy in a Moon Rides T-shirt over and told him to man the controls. Then he led Darcy onto the wooden floor of the bumper car arena. "What's your favorite color?" he asked.

"For a car? Red," Darcy said. "Absolutely."

"Red it is." Daniel helped her into a bright red car and made sure the seatbelt was tight. "I'm going to go for black."

"Okay, but watch out," Darcy warned him. "I'm from California. People drive fast there!"

"Bring it on," he joked. "I'm a professional at these bumper cars."

When the power came on, Darcy spun the wheel toward Daniel's car and jammed her foot on the gas. She slammed right into him. Then she turned away and drove as fast as she could toward the other side of the arena. But Daniel was too fast for her. He came up behind her and smacked into the back of her car. He kept driving, pushing her forward and making her bang into a bunch of other people before she managed to steer clear of him. Darcy couldn't stop laughing. She hadn't had this much fun in years!

When the ride was over, Daniel met her at the side of the arena.

"That was some fancy driving," he teased.

"I just didn't want to make you look bad," Darcy teased back.

He looked right into her eyes. "You're too pretty to make anyone look bad, ever," he murmured.

Darcy's heart gave a little jump. He was perfect!

❋ DARCY'S DISH ❋

I am so serious. All Daniel has to do is look into my eyes and smile, and my heartbeat totally speeds up. He is so cool, and so cute! I still can't believe I met such a great guy out here in the middle of nowhere. Maybe moving to Bailey wasn't such a bad idea after all!

"Let's go play a game," Daniel said.

"But what about your father?" Darcy asked.

"We'll stay nearby. He can still find me." Daniel grabbed her hand, and they made their way through the crowd to a little cluster of game booths about fifty feet from the bumper cars.

"Are you a professional at these games, too?" Darcy asked. "You must get so bored of this stuff with all the fairs you go to."

"I manage to keep myself busy," Daniel said. He stopped in front of a hoops game. "Which stuffed animal do you want?"

Darcy studied the animals hanging from the top of the booth. "I like that pink kitty," she said. "But it's one of the big ones."

The guy running the booth began to laugh.

"What's so funny?" Darcy asked.

He stopped laughing. "Nothing," he said. "Just . . . that's a tough one to get. You need five out of five baskets."

"No sweat." Daniel plopped down his money, and the guy handed him a basketball, shaking his head.

Daniel grinned at Darcy, then turned and shot the ball. One. Two. Three. Four. Five. He hadn't missed a single one!

"Looks like all your practice has paid off," the guy said, handing Daniel the big pink cat.

Daniel gave it to Darcy. "Your giant cat, my lady."

"Thank you," Darcy said, hugging it. "I love it!"

"Listen, I better get back to the bumper cars in case my dad is looking for me," Daniel said. They turned and began walking toward the rides.

"Later, Carter!" the guy at the booth called.

Darcy turned around in confusion. Who was he talking to? The booth guy was looking right at them. But Daniel was looking at *her*. He gazed right into her eyes, and her stomach did a flip-flop. "I wish I had more time to hang," he murmured. "I always have such a great time with you, Darcy."

"Me too," Darcy said. "With you, I mean."

"We'll definitely have plenty of time at the dance," Daniel said. "I can't wait."

"Me neither," Darcy said.

She walked Daniel to the bumper cars, then practically floated back to the Creature Comforts booth.

Jack sat at his makeshift table flipping through a deck of tarot cards. Lindsay was in her own little world, humming and sweeping the waiting area—with a rake, oddly enough—so she didn't notice Darcy come in.

"Um, Linds?" Darcy said as she set down her purse and the pink kitty-cat. "What is going on with you lately?"

"What do you mean?" Lindsay asked cheerfully.

Darcy grabbed the broom from behind the counter and held it up. "I know the floor of the booth is made of dirt. But raking it only makes the dirt stand up higher and get all over the place. That's why we use the push broom here."

Lindsay stared at her in surprise.

"I know," Darcy said. "Freaky, right? You doing something weird and me correcting you? It's a total role reversal."

"Wow, I guess I really am out of it," Lindsay said with a frown.

"No, don't be sad!" Darcy cried. "It's kinda fun, actually. But you have to tell me what's up. I feel like we've hardly talked all week."

"Well . . . I met a guy." Lindsay's face turned redder than her strawberry blond hair.

"No way!" Darcy said. She pulled out Jack's "customer chair" and took a seat. "Spill. I want all the details."

"He's really sweet, and he's really cute," Lindsay said. She blushed and hid her face in her hands. "I'm such a dork. This is why I didn't want to tell you."

"What?" Darcy cried. "You're not a dork! You're supposed to tell me stuff like that!"

Lindsay peeked out from between her fingers. "But I'm so embarrassed."

"Of course you are," Darcy said. "That's what happens when you like a guy. You get all embarrassed and excited and gooey."

"Really?" Lindsay looked up and smiled. "Then I guess I'm normal."

Darcy laughed. "You? Normal? No one would believe it," she joked. Lindsay was, hands-down, the most normal person she'd ever met. "So what else? Tell me about him."

"Well, I think he really likes me," Lindsay said. "He told me he's never met anyone like me before— he loves how serious and responsible I am."

"Even when you're acting like a total dork and sweeping with a rake?" Jack asked skeptically.

Darcy ignored him. "What else?"

"Ooh, he won me a stuffed animal today." Lindsay pulled a big pink cat out from behind the counter.

"I can't believe it!" Darcy jumped up and grabbed her own pink cat. "I met a guy, and he won me the exact same thing!"

"You met a guy?" Lindsay cried. "Why didn't you tell me?"

"Uh, because I was embarrassed," Darcy said. "Just like you. I thought you'd make fun of me."

"No way," Lindsay said. "I'm psyched for you."

They bounced up and down and squealed with excitement.

Jack rolled his eyes. "The Great Jacktoni predicts that you're both going to become even more annoying before this conversation is over," he said.

"And the best part is that he asked me to the dance on Saturday," Lindsay went on. "I've never had an actual date for the state-fair dance before!"

"My guy asked me to the dance, too!" Darcy cried. "This is so cool. I can't believe we both met boys! Where does yours—"

"Guinea pigs coming through," a voice interrupted them. Darcy turned to see a middle-aged woman pulling an entire wagon full of guinea pigs. "I need checkups and shots for all of them. They're the class pets for the entire school," she explained.

"Then we'd better get started," Lindsay said, all business. She handed the woman a form to fill out and went into the back to get her father.

Darcy sighed. Shouldn't these guinea pigs be at a guinea pig race or something? So much for their slow day at the fair!

Chapter 6

Wild Wisdom . . . *The marine iguana of the Galápagos Islands can stay underwater for about half an hour.*

On Thursday morning, Darcy was surprised to find her mother all decked out like Lara Croft, complete with a pith helmet.

"Don't tell me," Darcy quipped. "You're sick of living on the ranch, and now you've decided to move us to the jungle? Or wait, does that outfit belong on safari?"

Victoria smiled and shook her head. "This outfit is for hunting," she said. "Spider hunting."

Darcy raised an eyebrow. "How big *are* these spiders?"

"Oh, they can reach up to an inch and a half long," Victoria answered seriously.

"Better bring a tranquilizer gun," Darcy joked. She poured herself a bowl of cereal and began chomping away. She wondered what she and Daniel would do at lunch today. Maybe they could head over to the horse section of the fair and take a pony ride. Or better yet, an actual horse ride, with both of them on the same horse. It would be so romantic!

"You know, I'm sure Kevin would let you take the morning off if you want to help us," Victoria said.

Darcy almost choked on her cereal. Skip the fair? Maybe miss out on seeing her adorable sort-of boyfriend? And for *spiders*? "Um . . . no thanks," she mumbled through a mouthful of food.

"Oh, come on. Wouldn't you like to get out there and face down nature?" Victoria dropped into an action-heroine pose, as if she were pointing a huge gun at a dinosaur or something. Darcy grinned. Her mother had certainly played her share of action girls in the movies.

"Mom, you're totally against harming anything in nature, and you don't believe in guns," Darcy pointed out.

"True." Victoria dropped her pose and perched on one of the barstools. "Eli and I are planning to capture the spiders in jars. We're going to need a lot of jars, though—one per spider. If we put in more than one, they might get uppity and eat each other!"

"Charming," Darcy said.

"I think it's going to be quite fascinating, actually," Victoria told her. "Wolf spiders make these burrows for themselves, so they're very hard to find. You have to look for the turrets."

"Turrets?" Darcy repeated. "The spiders have houses with turrets?"

"Oh, yes. They make them from leaves and pine needles, and they tie them all together with spider silk." Victoria's eyes shone.

"Mom, don't take this the wrong way, but you need to get out more," Darcy said.

Victoria smiled. "Well, I am planning to go to the dance on Saturday. So I will be getting out."

Darcy's heart sank. She didn't particularly want her mother at the dance while she was trying to have a romantic evening with Daniel. "You're not planning to hang out with me, are you?" she asked. "I mean, not for the whole time?"

"Heaven forbid," Victoria said. "I'll only swing by once in a while so you can do a lipstick check for me."

Darcy smiled. "As long as you do a lip-gloss check for me."

"It's a deal," Victoria told her. "We'll both have beautiful lips all night long!"

Suddenly there was a loud crash from the front porch. Followed by another loud crash. And another.

"I do believe Eli is here," Victoria said, leading the way to the front door. She pulled it open . . .

. . . And there was Eli, on his knees amid a slew of glass jars. The jars rolled all over, heading in every direction. Eli scrambled to grab them all and stop them from rolling. But every time he got one, another one went rolling by. Three of them had already rolled down the steps and broken.

"I think we're going to need some more jars," Victoria said wisely.

"Thank you so much for helping me, Lindsay," Kathi whispered. "I stink at dog training. The only way I can get Skittles to listen to me is by yelling in this really deep voice. But now I'm totally hoarse from yelling, and she won't obey me at all when I whisper at her."

Lindsay nodded. She'd agreed to spend the morning at the Giraldis' car booth, helping Kathi train Skittles for the talent show on Saturday. Darcy was manning the Creature Comforts booth.

"Why are you using a deep voice?" she asked Kathi.

"That guy Mikey said I have to be the alpha dog," Kathi explained. "You know, the top banana. But I don't think Skittles is buying it."

Lindsay nodded. "Mikey is right. You have to be the one in charge. In the wild, dogs would live in packs, and one dog would be the leader. All the other dogs would listen to that top dog. So you have to be the top dog, and Skittles will listen to you. But it doesn't mean you have to yell."

"I don't know how else to be commanding," Kathi croaked.

"Well, you just have to believe that you're in charge," Lindsay tried to explain. "If you expect Skittles to listen to you, she will."

Kathi wrinkled her nose. "I'm not so great at being in charge," she admitted. "You're really good at it. Maybe you can go to the talent show with Skittles. You can be her official coach!"

"No thanks," Lindsay said. "I'm going to be busy before the dance on Saturday." *Busy getting ready for my date with Carter,* she added silently, her heart doing a happy little bounce.

Kathi narrowed her eyes. "Busy how?" she asked suspiciously.

Busted! Lindsay's cheeks grew hot. "Um . . . I sort of . . . have a date," she admitted. "For the dance."

Kathi's mouth fell open. "You too?" she asked. "Am I the only dateless one?"

Lindsay bit her lip. "You heard about Darcy's guy?"

"Yes." Kathi thought about it for a moment, then smiled. "And I'm totally happy for both of you!"

"Thanks, Kath." Lindsay sighed with relief. "But it means I can't spend all my pre-dance time with Skittles. And besides, you entered Skittles in the talent show so that you would have something to do. It's not going to help if I do it for you."

"You're right," Kathi said. "I just don't know how to be commanding."

"Make believe you're a queen," Lindsay said. "And you're talking to your servant."

Kathi stood up straight and tall and lifted her chin high in the air. She looked down at Skittles with her adorable wrinkled face . . . and burst out laughing. "I can't think of Skittles as a servant," she giggled. "What would she be? Chief of face-licking?"

"Okay, then pretend you're the CEO of a big company and you're talking to your assistant," Lindsay said.

Kathi frowned. "I'm not sure what that means."

"Then pretend . . ." Lindsay searched her brain for another idea. "I know! Pretend you're Darcy's mother in that movie—the one where she plays the queen of the jungle. You know, and all the animals worship her and do whatever she says."

"I love that movie!" Kathi cried. "I can do that." She looked down at Skittles. "Skittles, up!" she commanded in an English accent.

Skittles cocked her head to one side, confused.

Lindsay tried not to laugh. "What was that?" she asked.

"Well, I'm being Darcy's mom," Kathi said. "She has an accent."

"Can you be Darcy's mom without the accent?" Lindsay asked.

Kathi considered it. "I don't think so," she said.

"Okay then," Lindsay said. "Skittles will just have to get used to it. Now remember, you're the queen of the jungle, and Skittles is one of your animal subjects."

"Skittles, up!" Kathi commanded.

Skittles raised her front paws in the air.

"Good!" Kathi cried. "Now Skittles . . . *dahnce*!" she ordered. She held her arms up like the pug's front paws, and danced in a circle, trying to show her what to do.

Skittles just sat back on her haunches and stared at Kathi as if she were crazy.

"Maybe we can teach her to sing instead," Lindsay said helplessly.

"I see a man in your future," Jack said in a deep voice. "Tall, dark, kinda handsome. You will fall madly in love with him."

Darcy winced. In between patients at the booth, she'd been watching Jack tell fortunes for the people who trickled in. And he said that same thing to every single woman or girl who sat down at his table.

"I'm married!" this particular woman snapped. "I'm not going to fall madly in love with some strange man." She began to stand up.

"Well, maybe it's not a man," Jack protested. His voice went back to normal as he scrambled to find an excuse. "Maybe it's a . . . a . . . horse. Or a dog or a cat. You know, a male animal that's big and has dark fur."

The woman raised an eyebrow.

"The cards are not an exact science. Sometimes my visions cannot be taken at face value," Jack explained in his deep Great Jacktoni voice.

❋ (DARCY'S DISH) ❋

You should see Jack reading the tarot cards. It's hilarious! It's so obvious that he has no idea what any of them mean. You remember all the parties in Hollywood that had fortune-tellers as part of the entertainment? Well, even I managed to pick up a little about reading tarot cards—enough to realize that Jack's tarot cards should all be faceup. At this one reading, he had two of the seven of them facing down so that you couldn't even see the picture! And he never bothers to explain the difference between a card whose picture is facing the customer and a card whose picture is facing him. I'm no fortune-teller, but I know from experience that the way tarot cards are laid out is very important in reading their meanings. But the Great Jacktoni is just making it up as he goes along! I mean, I tried to explain it all to him—you know, about the different meanings of the cards and all. But he just waved his little hand at me and told me it didn't matter. I just hope his customers agree!

"Okay, what else?" the woman asked.

"I see a lot of money," Jack said. "You will be rich."

"That doesn't seem very likely," the woman said skeptically. "Where in the cards does it say that?"

"Oh, uh . . ." Jack looked at the cards, then grabbed one that had a skeleton on it. "Right here! See, this means you're going to start a successful career as a mortician."

"That's ridiculous," the woman said. "You're a

fraud." She got up and stormed off into the aisle.

"Tell all your friends to come to the Great Jacktoni!" Jack called after her.

Darcy shook her head. "Jack, did you even read the instructions that came with those tarot cards?"

"Instructions are for losers," Jack said. "I'm doing fine without them."

"No, you're not. She just called you a fake," Darcy pointed out.

"Yeah, but she didn't ask for her money back," Jack said. "That's all that matters."

"I hear you, little man," Alex said, wandering over from the Wave of the Future booth. "You have to be harsh when it comes to business. It's all about the bottom line."

"Dude, you don't even know what that means," Mikey complained, following his twin over to the Creature Comforts booth. "What's the bottom line?"

"It's just an expression," Alex said. "Isn't it?"

Darcy shrugged. "You got me. How's it going over there?"

"It's pretty bodacious," Mikey said. "Remember that guy who came by yesterday?"

Darcy nodded. "He looked like a surfer dude waiting to happen."

"He totally was," Mikey replied, a huge grin on his face. "He came back this morning with, like, five friends and they all tried out the Simu-Surfer."

"That's amazing!" Darcy cried. And it was—it was the best news she'd heard all day. Mikey and Alex were kind of crazy with their fake surfer talk, but they seemed like really sweet guys underneath it all. And she had to respect anyone who insisted on surfing even though the ocean was a thousand miles away. "I'm so happy for you guys."

"Okay, Darcy, Bitsy is ready to go back to her owner," Kevin called from the back.

"Sorry," Darcy told Mikey and Alex. "Duty calls." She went in and picked up Bitsy—an enormously fat tabby cat—in her arms.

"You're going to have to hang out here for a while, kitty," Darcy told her. "Your people are busy going on carnival rides." As she put Bitsy into one of the cat crates they'd lined up inside the counter, Darcy pictured the carnival rides . . . and the very cute boy who was probably running one of them right this very second! She wished Daniel had a cell phone so she could send him a text message. But he said his father didn't believe anyone under the age of eighteen needed a cell phone.

She could just imagine how her friends in Los Angeles would respond to that one!

Kevin came out of the examination area, yawning. "Busy morning," he said. "Who's next?"

"We don't have any patients signed up," Darcy told him. "I think everybody's eating lunch around now. Maybe it will pick up again in the afternoon."

"Well, why don't you go eat, too?" Kevin said. "I'll stay here and watch the booth in case we get any stragglers."

"No way, dude," Mikey put in. "I already ate lunch. I'll watch your booth for you. You can both go grab some chow."

"Really?" Darcy asked.

"Yeah. I know the drill," he said. "Somebody comes in with a pet, I take down their name and what they need done. Then I tell them to come back in half an hour after the doc's had time to eat. Right?"

"Right," Kevin said.

"I've been watching Darcy in action," Mikey said, giving her a wink. "It will be no problem."

"Thanks," Darcy said. "Kevin will be back in half an hour, and Lindsay should show up sometime soon. She's been dog-training all morning."

Mikey nodded. He jumped up onto the counter,

swung his legs over, and jumped down on the other side.

"I really appreciate this," Darcy told him. "I'm starving." *And I can't wait to see Daniel,* she thought.

"Hey, what are friends for?" Mikey said.

"I'll be back in an hour," Darcy told him. "Call my cell phone if you need me." She jotted down the number at the top of the patient sign-in sheet.

"Get out of here!" Mikey said. "Have a fun lunch."

Darcy took off. When she found Daniel near the rides, she already had a plan in mind. "Swimming pigs," she told him.

"Is that how you guys say hello in Hollywood?" Daniel asked.

"No, we say *'flying* pigs,' " Darcy joked. "I thought we could catch the next show."

"You really want to see the swimming pigs? We could swing by the music stages instead. Check out one of the live bands," Daniel said.

"Nope. I didn't know pigs could swim, and I'm not gonna believe it until I see it with my very own eyes," Darcy said.

Daniel held out his hand. "Then swimming pigs it is."

They made their way across the fairgrounds to the livestock section. In the center was a five-foot-deep pool with a little diving platform sticking out over the edge. Darcy and Daniel sat on the bleachers and ate popcorn while four pigs trotted out onto the platform, jumped into the water, and swam in a series of intricate patterns.

"They swim like dogs!" Darcy cried. "How do they know how to do all those fancy moves?"

"This guy named Billy trains them," Daniel told her. "I've seen him at a couple of different fairs. He says the pigs are really smart. They're easier to train than dogs."

"Hmm. Who knew?" Darcy said.

One of the pigs swam right by her, close enough that she could almost touch it. Darcy could hardly believe she was having so much fun watching a bunch of farm animals. Of course, the cute guy sitting next to her certainly helped make the whole thing even more enjoyable.

Darcy leaned over to talk into his ear. "I told you this would be fun," she said. "I bet you never thought swimming pigs could be a cool date activity."

"But you've proven it to me," he said. "Pigs are very romantic."

When the show was over, they wandered through the fair, taking the long way back to Darcy's booth.

"Hey, check it out!" Darcy cried as they passed an old-fashioned game booth. "It's whack-a-mole."

"Wait, you've never had a corn dog, but you recognize whack-a-mole?" Daniel asked.

"I went to this really lame party once when I was, like, eight," Darcy said. "We went to the Santa Monica Pier, and it was so windy that all the rides were closed, and all we could do was play games all day. They had about four whack-a-mole places and some kind of bowling game."

"So you played whack-a-mole," Daniel guessed.

"Yup. I was the total champion." Darcy dug in her purse and pulled out a dollar. "What stuffed animal do you want?" she asked, just like Daniel had asked her yesterday.

He raised his eyebrows. "The snake, I guess. Do you really think you can win it?"

"Watch and learn," Darcy joked. She handed over her dollar, grabbed the stick, and waited for the first little robot mole head to pop out of a hole. As soon as it did, she bopped it with her stick. Then another, and another, and another. She grinned as she played. This was a skill that hadn't come in very handy in Beverly Hills, but it sure was fun here! When the moles stopped jumping up, Darcy checked her score.

"The lady wins," said the woman behind the game. "What do you want?"

"The stuffed snake," Darcy told her. She took her prize and handed it over to Daniel. "See. Now we each have a souvenir."

"Cool." He grinned. "Nobody's ever won *me* a stuffed animal before." He draped the snake over his shoulders and took Darcy's hand. "Come on, let's go get some cotton candy. Do they have that in Malibu?"

"They have cotton candy everywhere," Darcy told him.

He bought a cone at one of the vending carts, and they shared it as they wandered back toward the Creature Comforts booth. "I've never even seen where you work," Daniel said. "Which one is it?"

"The one with the hay bales in front and the sign for the Great Jacktoni," Darcy said, pointing. She was happy to see Lindsay standing behind the counter, helping a guy with a Dalmatian. She had been worried that Lindsay would be stuck training Skittles all day long. "And that's my best friend, Lindsay," she added.

Daniel dropped her hand. His face was white. "Oh. Cool," he said. "Um, listen, I'd better get back to the bumper cars." He turned his back on the Creature Comforts booth.

Darcy looked at him, surprised. They were still fifty feet from her booth. "I thought you were going to walk me back," she said.

He shot a glance over his shoulder at Lindsay and the booth. "Well, you're almost there, right?" he snapped.

Darcy's mouth fell open. Daniel had never been so harsh before. What was wrong with him? Had she offended him somehow? "I guess," she squeaked.

Daniel stepped away so that an ice-cream cart was between him and the Creature Comforts booth. "I just don't want my dad to get mad at me for being gone so long," he said in a more normal tone. He gave her one of his dazzling smiles. "See you tomorrow?"

"Sure," Darcy said. He took off before she could even thank him for the cotton candy.

She watched him go, confused. Up until now, he'd been so nice all the time. But that little episode had been seriously weird. Why didn't he want to walk her to her booth? With a shrug, she turned and headed slowly back to work.

"Hi, Linds," she said. "How was the dog training?"

"Exhausting," Lindsay said. "Even when Kathi gets the whole command voice down, Skittles still isn't very good at standing on her hind legs. She's just a top-heavy dog."

"Maybe Kathi should train her to do something else," Darcy said.

"I know. But when I suggested that, Kathi didn't even want to think about it," Lindsay said. "She has her heart set on Skittles the dancing dog."

Darcy laughed. "Did you get back while Mikey was watching the booth?" she asked.

"Yeah. What was that all about?" Lindsay asked.

"He's so nice. He offered to do it so your dad and I could take lunch," Darcy said. "How did he do?"

"My father wants to hire him full-time," Lindsay joked. "He created a whole new inventory checklist, and he even swept the floor."

"Hmph. He's trying to make me look bad," Darcy said with a smile.

"Listen, do you mind if I take lunch right away?" Lindsay asked. "I'm starving."

"Not at all," Darcy said, giving her a wink. She knew Lindsay was going to go find the boy she'd been seeing.

"Thanks." Lindsay beamed. She grabbed a cute beaded purse Darcy had never seen before, ran a hand through her hair—which was down again—and skipped off into the crowd.

"She's being weird lately," Jack commented from his

perch at the fortune-telling table.

"I think it's nice to see her all happy," Darcy told him. She checked out Jack's grumpy expression. His turban was on crooked, and his tarot cards were scattered all over the table. "Is business not going well today?" she asked.

"I had a huge line while you were at lunch," Jack replied. "But none of them seemed to like their fortunes. I'm beat." He pulled off his robe and draped it over the Great Jacktoni sign. "I need a big pretzel to recharge."

Darcy watched him go, then turned to check the patient sign-in list. They had a cat, two dogs, and an iguana waiting for checkups. She glanced in at Kevin, who was quickly cleaning the examination table with a disinfectant wipe. He gave her a thumbs-up.

"Okay, Kitty Foo-Foo is next," Darcy called. "Come on in!"

By the time she was finished helping Kevin with all their clients, Lindsay's lunch hour was over. She came wandering up, finishing a cone of cotton candy, with a dreamy look in her eyes.

"Want some?" Lindsay asked, holding out the cotton candy.

Darcy clutched her stomach. "No thanks. I had a

bunch before. I'll go into sugar overload if I eat any more."

"I had the best time," Lindsay said, lowering her voice. The Great Jacktoni had a client, but Darcy knew they had to keep him from listening in and hearing too much about either of their boyfriends. It was no fun to be teased by a little kid. Especially a smart little kid like Jack, who would know all the most embarrassing things to say.

"What did you guys do?" Darcy asked.

"The weirdest thing," Lindsay said. "We went to see the swimming pigs show. You wouldn't think that would be a good date, but it was really fun."

Darcy felt a strange prickling sensation at the back of her neck. "Pigs are very romantic," she murmured, remembering Daniel's joke.

"Yeah, that's what he said!" Lindsay stuffed some cotton candy in her mouth.

"And then he bought you cotton candy," Darcy said.

"Yup."

"Did he walk you back here?" Darcy asked, peering around.

"No. He kinda dropped me off halfway down the aisle," Lindsay said. "Why?"

"Yesterday he won you a cat. Did he win it at one

of those basketball games?" The strange feeling on Darcy's neck was now running all up and down her spine.

"Yeah." Lindsay narrowed her eyes. "What's up with you?"

"Does your guy work at the bumper cars?" Darcy whispered, not really wanting to hear the answer.

"No," Lindsay said.

Relief filled Darcy's body.

"He works at the Whip," Lindsay went on. "His dad runs it."

The relief drained out of Darcy. "The Whip?" she said.

Lindsay's brow furrowed. "What is it?"

"The guy I'm dating works at the bumper cars, but his father also runs a few other rides," Darcy said. "Maybe even the Whip."

"So they're probably friends," Lindsay said.

"Maybe," Darcy said. But she couldn't help remembering how bizarre Daniel had acted before when he dropped Darcy off at the Creature Comforts booth. He'd practically run in the other direction. "What's his name? I never even asked."

"Carter," Lindsay said.

Alarm bells went off in Darcy's head. Carter.

That's what the guy at the hoops game had called Daniel the other day. Well, he'd called someone by that name, and Daniel had been the only guy around.

"My guy's name is Daniel," Darcy said. "Is Carter his first name? It kinda sounds like a last name."

"I never asked. He introduced himself as Carter, so I figured it was his first name." Lindsay studied her. "Wait a minute. What are you thinking?" she asked.

"I just can't help wondering if they're the same guy," Darcy said. "I guess that's stupid, huh? But we had the exact same date with our guys."

"So what?" Lindsay said. "If they're friends, they probably talked about fun things to do."

"You're right," Darcy told her. "But still. . . . What does Carter look like?"

"He has green eyes and dark hair cut short," Lindsay said.

"So does Daniel," Darcy said.

"So?" Lindsay shook her head. "You're crazy. Half the guys at the fair have dark hair."

That was true. But Darcy couldn't get over the uneasy feeling she had. If Daniel had seen Lindsay and knew she was dating his friend, he would have just told Darcy that. He wouldn't have taken off as if he'd seen a ghost! And that guy at the booth had definitely used the name Carter. She had to get to the bottom of this.

"Hey, Mikey!" she yelled across the aisle.

He stuck his head out of the Wave of the Future booth. "Wassup?"

"Can you watch the booth for us again? Just for ten minutes?" Darcy asked.

Mikey wandered across the aisle. "*No problemo.*"

"Thanks. We owe you." Darcy grabbed Lindsay's hand and pulled her out into the aisle.

"Where are we going?" Lindsay cried.

"To the bumper cars," Darcy told her. "And if that doesn't work, to the Whip."

"I'm telling you, you're insane," Lindsay insisted as Darcy towed her through the crowd. "You are totally paranoid."

"I know," Darcy admitted. "Just humor me."

Lindsay sighed and shook her head.

Darcy stopped short about ten feet from the bumper cars. "We need some cover," she said. "I don't want him to see us."

"Oh, come on," Lindsay protested. "You think he's going to run and hide?"

"Doesn't it seem weird to you that neither of our

guys would come near the Creature Comforts booth?" Darcy said. "He doesn't want us to find out that he's seeing us both."

"You're imagining things," Lindsay said. But she didn't sound very confident.

"There! The living statue," Darcy cried. She pointed to a Statue of Liberty standing outside the line for the bumper cars. It wasn't a real Statue of Liberty. It was a woman dressed up in a green outfit with green makeup on her face, acting like the Statue of Liberty. Darcy had never seen her move a muscle—she was really good!

"We can hide behind her," Darcy said, creeping over to Lady Liberty. "He won't notice us."

"Carter doesn't even work here," Lindsay said. "So I don't see why we have to hide."

Darcy ignored her and crept right up to the living statue. She stood about a foot away, pulling Lindsay in close to her. Then she leaned over and peeked under Lady Liberty's raised arm.

Daniel was working the switch for the bumper cars, looking as cute and friendly as ever.

"There!" Darcy whispered. "At the controls. That's Daniel."

Lindsay peeked around her, squinting to see the

guy at the controls. "That's Carter!" she gasped.

"Do you mind?" a voice said.

Darcy jumped. She looked up—and saw the Statue of Liberty frowning down at them. "You're a little close," the statue said.

"Sorry." Darcy stepped back, knocking into Lindsay. "We just caught both our boyfriends—well, our *boyfriend*—in a big lie!"

"Really? What a jerk," said Lady Liberty. Then she put herself back in her statue pose and stopped moving again.

Darcy headed quickly up the aisle, wanting to get out of sight of the bumper cars. Lindsay followed more slowly.

"I can't believe it," Lindsay said when she caught up. "Are you saying . . . do you mean . . ."

"Yes. It's absolutely true. We're dating the same boy!" Darcy cried.

Chapter 7

Wild Wisdom . . . *Unlike most spiders, the wolf spider does not spin a web! Instead, it hunts at night for food.*

❋ DARCY'S DISH ❋

Can you believe it? My perfect, sweet, sort-of boyfriend is really a two-timing jerk! Lindsay was practically hyperventilating! But after two minutes she totally snapped back into control. I was so proud of her. She knew just what to do. She went straight back to the hoops game and asked the guy about Daniel. Brilliant, isn't she? The hoops guy said he's seen Daniel around at a lot of the fairs and that he's always with a new girl. He said everyone at the fair calls him by his middle name—Carter—because his dad's name is Daniel, too. I guess it gets confusing. So long story short, Mr. Daniel Carter Moon is a huge liar! And here I was, having such a great time at the fair. Now the whole thing is ruined—all because of a boy!

❋   ❋   ❋   ❋   ❋   ❋

"Want some more mint-chip ice cream?" Darcy asked that evening. Lindsay had come to sleep over, and they were both decked out in sweats and T-shirts while they sat around in the living room.

"I think I already ate too much." Lindsay groaned.

"I'll take some more," Jack said. He held out his bowl to Darcy.

"Just who invited you to our self-pity party?" Darcy asked, scooping him some more ice cream.

"Victoria. She says I'm always welcome here," Jack told her.

"Leave it to my mom," Darcy said.

"Besides, I'm supposed to practice my fortune-telling on her." Jack frowned. "Where is she, anyway?"

"She's out in the garden with Eli, releasing the wolf spiders," Darcy said. "Apparently they're nocturnal, so they have to be set free at night."

"Then I'll just have to practice on you two." Jack pulled his pack of tarot cards out of his jeans pocket. "I must be doing something wrong."

"Why?" Lindsay asked.

"Half my customers demanded their money back today." Jack shuffled the cards, then laid them out on the coffee table. "Okay, who's first?"

"You can't lay out the cards before you even know whose fortune you're telling," Darcy protested. "The cards are supposed to be charged by the energy of the specific person they're being read for."

"All right, all right," he said, exasperated. He stuck the cards back in the deck. "Lindsay, you first."

"Fine." Lindsay sat next to him on the couch. "But I don't want to hear anything about my future love life. Or my current love life, either."

Jack snorted. "As if." He pulled seven cards from the deck and slapped them onto the table. "Okay." He studied the cards, frowning and stroking his chin while he tried to look thoughtful. "Very interesting. I see that you're going to take a great journey. The vacation of a lifetime!"

"That sounds good." Lindsay perked up a little. "Where am I going to go?"

"Far, far away," Jack said.

"Where?"

"Um . . ." Jack looked panicked for a moment. "To an exotic locale."

"I know, but where?" Lindsay asked again.

"Bombay!" Jack cried.

Lindsay's eyebrows drew together in confusion. "Bombay?"

"No, uh . . . Botswana," Jack quickly corrected himself.

"Botswana? That's ridiculous," Lindsay said.

"Why would I go to Botswana?"

"For the fabulous nightlife," Jack told her.

"Wrong." Lindsay slumped back on the couch. "I'd ask for my money back, too."

Jack shrugged and turned to Darcy. "Darcy's turn! Have a seat and cross my palm with green."

"I'm supposed to cross your palm with silver," Darcy said.

"Times have changed. Now it costs five dollars," Jack replied.

"I'm not paying you to practice your fortune-telling on me." Darcy sat down and looked him right in the eyes.

"Oh, all right," Jack grumbled. He shuffled the cards again, then laid them out on the coffee table. He did his concentrating-hard thing, then sat back with a big smile on his face.

"What?" Darcy asked.

"You're going to become rich and famous," Jack said.

"Really? Cool!" Darcy cried. "I already know how to live that life, thanks to my mom. So I'm going to be an actor?"

"Absolutely," Jack said. "You'll live in Beverly Hills and go to all the big movie premieres, and you'll even win an Oscar."

"I can't believe it!" Darcy squealed. "That's exactly how I always pictured my life!"

"Great. So *you* wouldn't want your money back, right?" Jack asked.

"No way," Darcy said. "You totally nailed my future."

"He did not." Lindsay frowned at her brother. "All you did was tell her what she wanted to hear."

"Oh." Darcy crossed her arms and stared Jack down. "Is that true?"

"Yeah, and it worked," Jack said. "I knew I was good at this!"

"Wait a minute," Darcy protested. "The only reason that worked with me is because you know me, and you know what I want to hear. But your customers are total strangers. How are you going to figure out what they want to hear?"

"I don't know," Jack admitted.

"You can't do it that way, Jack," Lindsay said. "You have to really learn how to tell fortunes."

"Yeah," Darcy said. "I *do* want my money back."

"You didn't pay me," Jack pointed out.

"So?"

"Okay, let me try again," Jack said. "I won't just tell you what you want to hear. I promise." He examined the cards. "I've got it! I see it now. You're going to become rich and famous."

Darcy sighed. "How?"

"You will become the highest-ranked quarterback in the NFL," Jack told her.

"That's it," Lindsay said. "You're the worst fortune-teller in the world."

"Let's go check on my mom," Darcy suggested. "We could use a change of scenery."

She led the way outside to the vegetable garden. Victoria was still dressed in her hunting outfit, but her pith helmet was gone. Dirt was smeared all over the knees of her khakis, and her hair was a total mess.

"How's the spider festival?" Darcy asked.

"Awful," Victoria replied. "They won't leave their jars." She pointed her big flashlight down at a glass jar. Darcy leaned over to look at the big hairy brown spider inside. The light reflected from a bunch of eyes in the center of its head.

"Whoa," she said. "I'm not sure I want that guy out and about."

"Actually, that's not a guy," Eli said. He held two more jars in his hands. "The males are pretty small. We tried to capture mostly females. They're easier to find because they're much bigger."

Jack yawned. "I don't think you need me for this," he said. "I'm gonna head home. I have to get plenty of sleep so my psychic abilities will be sharp tomorrow."

Lindsay and Darcy just shook their heads as he wandered off toward his bike.

"I've got to get the spiders into the garden," Victoria said. "Those wretched beetles will ruin it otherwise."

"Maybe you should turn out the flashlights," Lindsay suggested. "If they're nighttime hunters, they might not like the lights."

"Wait, they actually hunt?" Darcy asked. "I thought spiders just made webs and waited for things to crawl into them."

"Not wolf spiders," Eli said. "They don't do webs. They just hunt down their prey, catch it, and eat it."

"Now I really don't want him—I mean her—out of the jar," Darcy said. "That thing is so big, she might try to hunt *me*!"

"Not with all these cucumber beetles around," Victoria said. "I believe Lindsay is right. We should turn off the flashlights. We'll just put the jars down, open them up, and leave them there. Hopefully the spiders will see the beetles, and then nature will take its course."

"We won't be able to see if the spiders go into the

garden," Eli pointed out. "They might just wander off into the fields. They don't know they're here to help the garden."

Victoria bit her lip as she thought about it. "I can't see any other choice," she said. "We'll just have to hope they go where the prey is." She took one of the jars from Eli, twisted off the top, and set it on the ground with the opening facing the vegetable garden.

Eli did the same with the other jar.

Lindsay grabbed a jar off the pile near the garden gate and headed a few feet away to put it down. Victoria raised her eyebrows at Darcy.

"Oh, all right," Darcy grumbled, grabbing a jar. "This day couldn't possibly get any worse anyway." She looked in at the huge spider. "Just don't bite me," she told it. She walked about fifteen feet away, opened the jar, and put it down on the ground.

Soon enough, all the jars were open. Without flashlights, it was impossible to tell if the spiders were coming out or not.

"I don't think there's anything else we can do tonight," Victoria said. "We'll just have to hope for the best."

"I'll head home, then," Eli said. "In the morning I can come back and pick up the jars."

"Good night. Thank you for all your help," Victoria told him.

"See ya, Eli," Darcy called. Lindsay waved. Then they both sighed, depressed again.

"Well. Shall we all go have a nice cup of cocoa?" Victoria said. Darcy and Lindsay trudged back inside with her and slumped at the kitchen table while Victoria put on water to boil. The spiders had been distracting and all, but they couldn't take Darcy's mind off of Daniel Carter Moon, and she knew Lindsay felt the same way.

"I can't believe he's such a jerk," Darcy said.

"I can't believe I thought he really liked me," Lindsay replied.

"Well, I thought he liked me, too. He said I was sophisticated," Darcy said.

"He said I was intellectual." Lindsay leaned her cheek on her hand. "It was your idea to go to the swimming pigs show, wasn't it?"

"Yeah. He thought it would be stupid, but we had lots of fun. I guess that's why he decided to take you there." She frowned. "But he won you the stuffed cat first, right?"

"It took him three turns to win it for me," Lindsay said sadly. "I thought it meant he really liked me."

"*That's* why the guy at the booth said he'd had a lot

of practice," Darcy realized. "He'd already spent all that time shooting hoops to win you a cat."

"He's been using one of us to get ideas on how to date the other one," Lindsay agreed. "That's really low."

"He seemed so sweet. How could he do this to us?" Darcy murmured.

"Now I won't really have a date for the dance," Lindsay said.

"Me neither," Darcy added.

"All right. That's it. I've heard enough," Victoria said. "Into the living room, now!"

Darcy gazed at her mother in surprise. "I thought we were having cocoa," she said.

"Talking first, cocoa later," Victoria replied. "Come on—chop, chop!"

Darcy dragged herself up and headed into the living room, with Lindsay trudging along behind her. They collapsed onto the couch, but Victoria stood in front of them, staring down at them with her hands on her hips.

"What?" Darcy asked.

"You two have been moping around ever since you got home from the fair today," Victoria said.

"We found out a boy was two-timing us," Lindsay said. "With each other!"

"It's the best reason to mope I've ever had," Darcy added. "I feel awful."

"Why?" Victoria asked. "Just because some boy is behaving rudely doesn't mean you girls have to feel bad about yourselves."

"But we thought he liked us," Lindsay said.

"We thought we had dates to the dance," Darcy said. "And now we're just . . . dateless and unliked."

"I like you," Victoria said. "And Kevin likes you. And Eli. And Jack. And—"

"Yeah, but it's not the same," Darcy said.

Victoria shook her head. "Now, girls, just think about it. Would you rather go to the dance with a boy who thinks he can treat you like this? Or would you rather go to the dance alone?"

Darcy bit her lip. Her mother was right—she wouldn't really want to go to the dance with Daniel now. Or with Carter. Or whatever his name was.

"I guess I'd rather go alone," Lindsay said. Darcy nodded.

"And why is that?" Victoria asked.

"Because now that I know that Daniel—Carter— isn't as cool as I thought he was, I don't really like him anymore," Darcy said. "I don't even know who he truly is—everything he said could be a lie."

"Exactly. And a boy who thinks he can lie to people doesn't deserve to have two wonderful girls like you moping around over him." Victoria turned back toward the kitchen. "I'm going to go get the cocoa."

Darcy turned to Lindsay and was surprised to see her friend sitting up straight and tall, with her arms crossed and the typical no-nonsense gleam in her eye.

"Your mother's right," Lindsay said.

"Yeah. She usually is," Darcy agreed.

"Carter doesn't deserve us," Lindsay said. "And you know what else he doesn't deserve?"

"What?"

"He doesn't deserve to get away with this," Lindsay said. "We need to teach him a lesson."

Darcy sat up, too. "Okay. So tomorrow we'll both go to the bumper cars—*together*—and we'll tell him we know what he's been up to. And we'll dump him!"

But Lindsay was shaking her head. "I have a better idea," she said.

Chapter 8

Wild Wisdom . . . *The pug is of Chinese origin, and these dogs lived in the lap of luxury as prized possessions of Chinese emperors. Sometimes, they even had their own soldiers guarding them!*

"I'm telling you, it will be fun," Lindsay said on Friday morning. Darcy was whipping up a batch of pancakes for breakfast because Eli had gone straight out to the garden to pick up the empty—hopefully!—spider jars.

"So we'll have him completely trapped," Darcy said. "And he'll be forced to confess."

"Exactly!" Lindsay raised her glass of orange juice in a toast.

"But—" Darcy began. Her words were cut off by a wail from outside. That could only mean one thing: Eli was in some kind of trouble.

They hurried outside and found Eli in the vegetable garden. Victoria came running out of the house a second later, still in the silk kimono that doubled as her bathrobe.

"Eli!" Victoria cried. "What on earth is wrong?"

"We've created a monster," he said, pointing to the garden. "Look!"

They all peered into the garden. There was no sign of the yellow-and-black beetles. But the ground seemed to be . . . moving.

"What is that?" Darcy asked, stepping closer for a better view.

"Spiders!" Eli cried. "Millions of them."

Darcy quickly stepped back. "What do you mean, millions of them?" she asked. "That's impossible."

"Okay, maybe not millions. But they're every-where," Eli moaned. "They've totally taken over."

"How could this happen?" Victoria asked. "We didn't release that many spiders last night."

"The only thing I can think is that we didn't notice their babies," Eli said.

Lindsay gasped. "They were all females!"

"Yeah, because they were easier to find," Eli said. "But female wolf spiders carry their young on their backs for a few days after they hatch. Then when they're big enough, they jump off and start living on their own."

"You mean that for every female spider we released, there were a bunch of other spiders we didn't see?" Victoria sounded a little freaked out.

Eli nodded solemnly. "They totally wiped out the cucumber beetles," he said helpfully.

"But now the garden is still out of balance," Victoria moaned. "All these spiders are going to be hunting. With so many of them, they're going to kill *all* the other insects in the garden!"

Darcy scrunched up her face in confusion. Why did her mother sound upset by that? "Um, wouldn't that be a good thing?" she asked. "We don't want all those bugs. Why not let the spiders eat them?"

"No, sweetheart, we *do* want those bugs," Victoria said. "There are many insects that are very beneficial to a garden. The trick is to keep them all in balance. And now we've gone and ruined that."

"What are you going to do?" Darcy asked.

Victoria sighed, taking in the creepy, crawly garden. "I just don't know."

"You're a lifesaver, Darcy!" Kathi cried later that morning. "I don't know what I would do without you. I mean, you always know just how to put an outfit together. Did they teach you that in school in California?"

Darcy couldn't help smiling. Kathi's boundless energy always cheered her up—and she needed cheering up today. Even though she and Lindsay had a

plan to teach Daniel Carter Moon a lesson, she still
felt down in the dumps. She had been having so much
fun at the fair with him, and now it all seemed like a
lie. She had a feeling that she'd remember this state
fair as being nothing but depressing.

She tried to shake off her thoughts of him and
concentrate on Kathi. Well, on Kathi and Skittles.

"It's not really an *outfit*," she said. "Just a tutu."

"And a crown," Kathi reminded her.

"A tiara," Darcy said. "I think a full crown would
be a little too much for Skittles." The pug whined as
if she agreed.

"Do you really think we'll find what we need
here?" Kathi asked. She looked around at the fabric
and textile booths with a doubtful look in her eyes.

"I've decided that this state fair has everything
in the world," Darcy said. "It's so much bigger and
more diverse than what I expected."

"Hey, Darcy!" called a kid on a skateboard. He
whipped past her so quickly that she couldn't even see
his face.

"Hey . . . you," she called back, shrugging at Kathi.

The skateboarder whirled around and sped back
over to them, kicking his board up and stopping right
in front of her. It was Alex.

"Oh, hi," Darcy said. "You're pretty good on the skateboard."

He nodded. "Mikey and I have both won championships. That's how we started teaching ourselves to surf—it uses a lot of the same moves as skateboarding." He reached down to scratch Skittles behind the ears.

"Hey, maybe you can teach Skittles to skateboard for the talent show," Darcy said, turning to Kathi.

But Kathi shook her head. "She's a ballerina. I just know it."

Alex shot Darcy a smile, and she grinned back. It was obvious to everyone that Skittles was not a ballerina—to everyone but Kathi.

"Hey, Alex, do you think I can come by later to try the Simu-Surf?" Darcy asked. "I have a friend I want to show it to."

"Lindsay?" he asked.

"Uh, no. Lindsay's already seen it, remember?" Darcy teased him. "It's someone else. But Lindsay will be there."

"Anytime, dude," he said. He kicked the board into position and took off. "See ya later," he called over his shoulder as he expertly wove through the crowd.

"Darcy, there it is!" Kathi cried. She rushed over to a booth labeled "The Tiny Dancer." It was stuffed with ballet supplies for little girls. "You were right. This will be perfect."

"Hi," Kathi said to the saleslady. "We need a tutu for my dog. Oh, and a tiara."

The saleslady drew back. "Excuse me?" she asked.

"Um, do you have dance outfits for babies?" Darcy translated for her friend. "We're looking for a teeny tiny tutu."

"Yes. I have five different tutus for very young babies," the woman said. "They're for dressing up only, of course. They aren't *real* tutus."

"Of course," Darcy agreed, keeping her voice very serious. This woman didn't seem to have much of a sense of humor, so Darcy figured serious was the way to go.

"We have pink, yellow, purple, pink *and* purple, or rainbow-colored." The woman pulled out all the little tutus and laid them out on her counter. Darcy examined the elastic waistbands—they were tiny. She glanced down at Skittles, who was scratching her ear so hard that she fell over sideways.

"I think these will fit," she told Kathi. "Which color do you like?"

"Oh, I don't know." Kathi bit her lip, looking from one to another. "The pink? No, wait. The yellow? No, wait—"

"How about the rainbow-colored one?" Darcy asked. "Skittles has enough personality to pull that off."

"Okay. The rainbow one," Kathi said.

The saleswoman looked disapprovingly at the dog, but she began wrapping up the rainbow tutu.

"And do you have a little tiara that would match?" Darcy asked. "Maybe one with multicolored gemstones?"

"Gemstones?" the woman repeated, astonished.

"No?" Darcy asked. "Okay, um, how about multicolored sequins?"

The saleswoman plucked a tiny tiara off a shelf. It was kind of hideous, Darcy had to admit—it had giant sequins in all different, way-too-bright colors. But it would certainly pop onstage. And Darcy had a feeling that the costume was all Skittles had going for her. She wasn't much in the talent department.

She glanced down at the pug. She was chewing on her own foot.

"She's going to be the best ballerina ever!" Kathi cried happily.

"Are you ready?" Lindsay asked at lunchtime.

"I guess so," Darcy said. "It's going to be hard to act normal around Daniel. I mean Carter. I'll have to use the acting skills I picked up from watching my mom in all those movies."

"Yeah, but won't it be fun to see him try to surf?" Lindsay asked.

"Do you really think he'll risk going so close to the Creature Comforts booth?" Darcy asked. "Do you think it will make him come clean about dating both of us?"

"There's only one way to find out." Lindsay gave her a thumbs-up.

Darcy headed off to the bumper cars, passing by the Statue of Liberty on the way. Daniel was waiting for her with his usual gorgeous smile.

Darcy took a deep breath. *He's a jerk,* she reminded herself. *No matter how cute his dimples are.* She pasted a smile on her own face.

"Hi," she said cheerfully. "Can you take a break?"

"For you? Absolutely," Daniel said.

Yesterday that would have made me feel special, Darcy thought. *Now he just seems kind of smarmy.* The realization made her happier. Daniel flagged one of his coworkers over to take his spot, and they started off down the aisle.

"Busy day at the bumper cars?" Darcy asked him.

"Yeah, there have been lines all day," Daniel replied. "It's always like this toward the end of the week."

"You've really been to a ton of these fairs, huh?" Darcy asked. "You must meet girls like me every time you go to a new place."

"No way," Daniel said. "I've never met anyone like you. You're the reason this fair has been so much fun."

I bet he'd say the same thing to Lindsay, Darcy thought. But she just acted like it was a sweet thing to say. If only she could make herself blush on cue like her mother could on film!

They were getting closer to the Creature Comforts booth. She saw Daniel realize where they were. He slowed down.

"Hey, do you want to go get something to eat?" he asked, reaching for her hand.

Darcy automatically pulled away. When Daniel frowned, she tried to cover by scratching her arm. "Um, no thanks," she said. "I actually have other plans for us today. I want to surf."

He laughed. "Good luck. You left the ocean behind in California."

"I know, but there's this superfun booth right across from mine," Darcy told him. "These two brothers have a machine that's like a surfboard on hydraulic lifts. It's really cool."

"Oh. But, you know, I don't really have that long . . ." Daniel said.

"I thought you told me you could take a break." Darcy put on her best pout. She kept walking toward her booth. Daniel inched along after her.

"Yeah, but I bet there's a line for the surfboard thing, right?" he said.

"I'm friends with the guys who run it," Darcy told him. "It will be no problem."

"It sounds like it will be boring for you, though," he said. He stopped walking again and gave her a serious, caring look. "You probably surfed all the time in California."

"But you've never surfed, have you?" she asked.

"No. But I don't want to make you do something that's boring just to make me happy," he said, sounding totally sweet and sincere.

He's a really good actor, Darcy thought. *He might be better than me!*

"I really miss surfing, actually," Darcy said. She began walking. They were only twenty yards from the

Creature Comforts booth, and she could see Lindsay at the counter inside, pretending not to watch them. "I'm dying to try it again."

Daniel wasn't following her. He stood still, looking nervous.

Darcy walked the few steps back to him. "Is something wrong?" she asked.

"No," he said quickly.

"Are you sure? Because you don't seem to be coming with me," Darcy pointed out.

"It's just . . ." Daniel's eyes darted back and forth. He was trapped.

Is he going to spill? Darcy wondered eagerly. *Is he going to tell me the truth?*

"What?" she prompted him.

He squared his jaw. "Nothing," he said. "Let's go." He grabbed her hand before she could stop him, and he started to run. He pulled her toward the Wave of the Future booth at top speed.

"Slow down!" Darcy called. Her cute little strappy sandals weren't made for sprinting.

But Daniel ignored her. He kept running until he reached the booth, then he ducked inside without ever turning his face toward the Creature Comforts booth.

Darcy glanced over her shoulder. Lindsay was

staring at them, her mouth open. Darcy shrugged, and Lindsay laughed.

"Okay, here we are," Daniel said breathlessly.

"Why did we have to run?" she asked.

"Oh . . . um . . . I just thought it would be fun and spontaneous," he said. "Just like you, Darce."

Sure you did, she thought.

"Darcy!" Mikey called from the back of the booth. "What up?"

"Not much," she replied. "Alex said I could come by for a ride, so here I am."

"Righteous," Mikey agreed. He looked at Daniel.

"Um, Daniel, this is Mikey," Darcy said. "Mikey, this is Daniel Moon."

"That's a pretty weird last name, dude," Mikey said. "Are you related to the Moon Rides guy? I heard he owns, like, half the rides here. Isn't his name Daniel Moon?"

"Yeah. He's my dad," Daniel told him.

Excellent! Darcy thought. She sent a silent thanks to Mikey for giving her an opening, even if it was accidental. "Wow, you have the same name as your dad?" she asked innocently. "Doesn't that get confusing?"

"Yeah." He laughed. "Most people call me by my middle name."

"Really? What is it?" she asked triumphantly.

His face went pale. She knew he was wondering if Lindsay had told her about this great guy named Carter that she was dating.

"It's, uh, Carter," he said. He studied her face for a reaction. Darcy forced herself to keep her expression neutral.

"Carter, huh?" she said. "I think I'll call you that from now on."

"O-okay," he replied, looking relieved.

Darcy hid a smile when she saw him shoot a glance out the doorway to the Creature Comforts booth.

"Are you here for the Simu-Surf, Carter Moon?" Mikey asked.

"I guess so." Carter looked doubtfully at the surfboard. "But maybe Darcy should go first. She's the expert."

Mikey nodded. "Hop on, Darce."

"Okay." Darcy took off her sandals and climbed onto the board. She scrunched her feet against it to get a feel for it. Then she bent her knees and leaned forward a little. "Go," she told Mikey.

He hit the remote control and the board rose up. It began moving slowly, just the way a real board would if you were riding a wave. Darcy swayed with the board, holding her arms out to the sides for balance.

Whenever the board changed directions, she adjusted her weight to compensate for it.

"Whoo-hoo!" Alex cried, coming into the booth. "Lookin' good, surfer girl!"

Darcy grinned. Now that she was up here, she realized she actually *did* miss surfing. In fact, with Mikey and Alex cheering her on and the wind in her hair, she was having a great time. The only thing that wasn't great about it was Daniel Carter Moon. He was watching her, his green eyes shining with admiration. But it was all fake. Or at least, it wasn't all *hers*. If Lindsay were on the surfboard, he'd be watching her the same way.

"Does it go any faster?" Darcy asked, looking away from Carter.

"Totally. Are you sure you can handle it?" Mikey asked.

"Yup. Bring it on!" Darcy cried.

Mikey hit another button on the remote, and the board started moving faster and higher. Darcy concentrated on the movements, imagining the hot California sun shining down on her and the gorgeous water of the Pacific below her board. She could almost smell the salt in the air, and she could picture the bluffs of Malibu perfectly. The faster the board moved, the faster she readjusted herself on it.

After a minute or two, Mikey hit the remote again and the surfboard slowed down. Darcy jumped off before it came to a complete stop.

"That rocked!" Alex cried. He gave her a high five.

"We should have had you in here the whole time, showing people how it's done," Mikey told her.

"Thanks." Darcy grinned. "That was the most fun I've had all week." And it was—even more fun than she'd had with Carter before she knew the truth about him. And speaking of Carter . . .

"Your turn," Darcy told him.

He looked alarmed. "I don't know if I can do that," he said.

"Sure you can," Alex said. "Hop on."

Carter stepped onto the board, still wearing his sneakers. He crouched down and nodded nervously at Mikey.

Mikey hit the remote, and the surfboard began to move. Carter tried to keep his balance, but he didn't look very graceful.

I have to get Lindsay now, Darcy thought. While Carter was busy concentrating on his surfing, she snuck out the entrance and rushed across the aisle. "Lindsay!" she called. "It's time!"

She could see it now: their total revenge. Mr.

Daniel Carter Moon wouldn't admit he was dating both of them, but how was he going to deny it when he was trapped on a surfboard with both Darcy and Lindsay standing between him and the door?

But Lindsay wasn't there.

Darcy hurried into the examination room. Lindsay was holding the head of a llama while Kevin prepared to give it a shot.

"Linds," Darcy hissed. "It's time!"

"Well, I can't go anywhere right now," Lindsay whispered, frustrated. "Stall him."

"I'll try," Darcy said. She ran back over to the Wave of the Future booth—just in time to see Carter fall off the surfboard.

"Whoa!" Mikey cried. He turned off the Simu-Surf. "You okay, dude?"

"Yeah." Carter climbed to his feet and gave Darcy a lopsided grin. "Guess I'm not as good as you," he said.

"Are you sure you're okay?" Darcy asked. She hadn't wanted him to get hurt.

"Sure, I'm fine," he said. "I think my ego might be bruised, though."

Darcy bit back a smile. If anybody's ego could stand to be bruised, it was his. "Do you want to try again?" she asked.

"No thanks," he replied. "I think I'm going to head back to the bumper cars where it's safe! See you later?"

Darcy glanced frantically at the Creature Comforts booth. There was still no sign of Lindsay. "Yeah," she said, frustrated. "See you later."

She watched him go, bummed. It looked as if she and Lindsay were going to have to come up with a Plan B.

It was a total downer. We had a whole plan worked out, and it was ruined by a llama. You'd be surprised how often that seems to happen in Bailey. But not to worry. Lindsay and I bounced right back with an even better get-Daniel-Carter-Moon plan. It's going to be the best revenge ever!

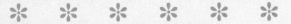

"I can't believe I missed the surfboard ride," Lindsay complained. "It would have been perfect! Carter surfing away as if everything is fine, then looking up to see you and me standing there and watching him . . ."

"It doesn't matter, Lindsay," Darcy told her. "Our new plan is a million times better anyway."

"I know." Lindsay sighed. "I just wanted it to be over with today."

"Well, tomorrow is close enough," Darcy said. She glanced at her watch. "The fair is closing in an hour. We'd better put this plan into action. Should I go first?"

"Yeah. Good luck," Lindsay told her.

Darcy left her booth and wound through the crowd until she got to the rides. Carter wasn't at the bumper cars. Luckily, thanks to Lindsay, she knew where to look next. She walked around the carousel and past the Ferris wheel until she got to the Whip.

Carter sat on a stool at the front of the line, taking tickets. Darcy went up to him, pasting a big smile on her face.

He looked shocked—and worried—when he saw her. "Darcy, hey!" he cried. "How did you find me here?"

She knew what he was thinking: *Did Lindsay tell you I work here?*

But Darcy just shrugged. "You weren't at the bumper cars, so I asked one of your coworkers."

"Oh." He relaxed. "Good thinking. So, what's up? Did you want to hang out for a bit?"

"No thanks," Darcy said. "I actually have to get back to work. I just wanted to say hi."

"Well, I'm glad you came by," Carter said. "Are you ready for the dance tomorrow?"

"Totally," Darcy said. "I'm going to find the perfect dress. I can't wait!"

"So when do you want to meet?" Carter asked.

"I was thinking seven o'clock," Darcy said. "Do you want to meet on the dance floor?"

Carter frowned. "It gets pretty crowded. Why don't we meet on one side of the floor. Say, the north side?"

"Sounds good," Darcy replied.

"Then it's a plan." Carter took a step closer to her.

"Great!" Darcy said quickly. "I'll see you then." She gave him a little wave and took off. She went back to the Creature Comforts booth.

Lindsay came rushing up to meet her. "What happened? How did it go?"

"I told him to meet me at seven," Darcy said. "He didn't suspect a thing."

"Okay, now it's my turn." Lindsay ran her hands through her hair, then stopped. "Wait a minute. Why am I trying to look good for that jerk?"

Darcy laughed. "You have to keep up appearances if you want to get our revenge."

"You're right. Meanwhile, I'll swing by the Brennan brothers' petting zoo on the way back," Lindsay said.

"We're going to need their help tomorrow if we want this plan to work."

Darcy nodded.

Lindsay didn't move. She looked a little nervous. "I haven't seen him all day. In fact, I haven't seen him since I found out he was two-timing us. I don't know if I can pretend to like him. What if I can't pull it off?" she asked.

"You can do it. Just smile and tell him you're psyched about the dance," Darcy coached her. "Then tell him to meet you at seven."

"But what if he says he can't?" Lindsay asked.

"He must have some kind of plan if he asked us both to the dance," Darcy said. "Ooh, and you know what? He wanted to meet me on the north side of the dance floor. I bet he tells you to meet him somewhere else."

"Maybe he thinks he can keep us separate and just keep leaving to get drinks or something," Lindsay said.

"I guess that could work . . . if we didn't know each other," Darcy said. "But we would've been hanging out together anyway."

Lindsay's pale skin was getting redder and redder. Darcy could tell she was angry. It was the perfect time for her to face Carter without being nervous. "Go do it," Darcy said. She pointed her friend toward the rides area and gave her a little push.

Lindsay stalked off like a soldier on a mission.

"Ice cream! Ice cream!" a shrill voice caught Darcy's attention. She turned to see a little girl leaping up and down over at Jack's fortune-telling station.

"No, sweetie, no more ice cream," the girl's frazzled mother was saying.

"Ice cream!" the girl shrieked.

"How could you do this?" the mother snapped at Jack. "She's already had so much sugar today that she won't sleep for a week!"

"I only say what I see in the cards," Jack said with a shrug.

"ICE CREAM!" The little girl stamped her feet.

"Fine. But only a small cone." The mother took her hand, glared at Jack, and stomped off toward the food court.

"What was that all about?" Darcy asked.

"I told her I saw an ice-cream cone in her future," Jack said.

"So now her mom has to buy her one." Darcy shook her head.

Jack grinned. "I've finally gotten the hang of this fortune-telling thing," he said. "It's like you said the other night—I know how to tell you what you want to hear because I know you. So I just have to pay a little attention to the customers and figure out what *they* want to hear."

"I thought you were doing that already," Darcy said.

"Nah. I was just saying things that *everybody* wants to hear," Jack said. "Like that you'll win money or go on vacation. The trick is to tailor it to each customer. That way, everyone is happy."

"That mother didn't look very happy to me," Darcy pointed out.

"She didn't ask for a refund," Jack said. "And as I told you before, that's all that matters!"

Lindsay jogged up to the booth, out of breath. "I did it!" She held up her hand for a high five.

Darcy slapped her hand. "Did he agree to seven o'clock?"

"He tried to weasel out of it and make it seven fifteen, but I pouted," Lindsay said. "So he said—and I quote—'I'll find some way to make it work.' "

Darcy giggled. "Girl, you're good!"

"He said to meet him at the south side of the dance floor," Lindsay said. "So you'll be on the north, and I'll be on the south."

"Let's just hope he doesn't have two other poor girls waiting on the east and the west," Darcy said.

Lindsay sat down on one of the folding chairs. "Tonight we have to pick out our dresses. And then it will be all set."

"The revenge-on-Daniel-Carter-Moon plan is on!" Darcy cried.

"What on earth is going on in here?" Victoria cried that evening. Darcy's room was covered with clothes, and she was giving Lindsay a fashion show. But one look around the room was enough for Victoria to see that it was a show of the ugliest fashions Darcy owned.

Darcy was wearing a bright orange miniskirt and a neon green tank with a strange little ruffle around the waist. "I'm trying to pick out an outfit for the dance tomorrow," Darcy said.

"Not that one," Lindsay told her.

Darcy disappeared into the closet.

"I don't understand," Victoria said. "I thought you had decided not to go to the dance with Carter. Or Daniel."

"We're not going with Daniel Carter," Lindsay told her.

"Ta-da!" Darcy cried. She came twirling back out of the closet wearing a hideous dress with stripes *and* polka-dots. "What do you think? With my giant purple plastic hoop earrings?"

"It's horrible," Lindsay gasped.

"I couldn't have said it better myself," Victoria agreed. "Wherever did you get such an ugly dress?"

"At this great little vintage store on Melrose," Darcy said. "My friends Keisha and Natalie were in a fight because Nat said Keisha's striped top was ugly. So then Keisha dissed Nat's polka-dotted bag. And they were totally not speaking to each other. So then I found this dress, and I wore it to school to prove to them that stripes and dots were *both* cool."

Lindsay wrinkled her nose as she studied the dress. "Did it work?"

"Well . . . kinda," Darcy said. "They both thought the dress was the ugliest thing they'd ever seen, so at least I got them to agree again."

Victoria smiled. "Then the dress served one good purpose. But it's far too ugly to wear again."

"Are you sure?" Darcy asked.

"Positive."

"Great! Then this is the perfect dress for the dance. Thanks, Mom!"

Chapter 9

Wild Wisdom . . . *The emu makes a loud booming call that is created by its large inflatable neck sac. The booming can be heard from more than a mile away.*

The doorbell rang at seven thirty on Saturday morning.

Darcy was standing in front of the refrigerator, gazing at the orange juice and the grapefruit juice. Nobody should be expected to make such difficult decisions this early in the morning.

The doorbell rang again, shaking her out of her trance.

"And nobody should be expected to receive visitors this early in the morning," Darcy muttered while she shut the fridge. She shuffled to the door in her bunny slippers and pulled it open to find the Brennan brothers standing there in overalls and big smiles.

"We're here with Captain Squawkers!" Brett announced.

"Oh, good," Darcy said. Then she took in the humongous parrot sitting on Brett's shoulder. "Wait. Why?" she asked.

"Because he loves to eat spiders," Victoria sang, coming downstairs in a pair of really cute overalls of her own. "Thank you, boys, for coming by so early on a weekend!"

"No problem. We're always up as soon as the first rooster crows," Brandon said.

"He doesn't understand the concept of daylight saving time, so he crows pretty early," Brett added.

Darcy rubbed some sleep from her eyes and looked at the three adults and the parrot. "Huh?" she asked.

"Apparently Captain Squawkers here has an absolute sweet tooth for spiders," Victoria said.

"We always thought parrots were vegetarians," Brett put in. "But they love the insects!"

"Not that spiders are insects," Brandon said quickly. "They're arachnids."

"And as you know, we have an overabundance of spiders in the vegetable garden," Victoria went on. "So my plan is to let the captain have a half hour in the garden. He can eat all the spiders he wants! Once the number of spiders is trimmed, they'll be back in balance with all the other bugs, and the garden will be safe!"

"Won't the spiders just make more spiders?" Darcy asked, confused.

"Most likely," Victoria said. "But then I'll just invite Captain Squawkers over for another snack."

"He never says no to a snack," Brett said. "Should we get started?"

"Absolutely." Victoria went outside and led him—and the parrot—over to the garden.

Brandon hung back. He gave Darcy a wink. "Our plan is still on for tonight, right?" he asked.

"You bet," Darcy said. "I can't wait!"

Holy cow! The fair is like a whole new place today. Huge crowds of people everywhere, carrying balloons, eating cotton candy, and grinning from ear to ear. You should see them! And I can hear people scream-ing all the way from the roller coaster. The whole place is totally filled with people talking and laughing and having the best time ever. Not me, though. For me it's all work. Our sign-up sheet is full for the day. Even Jack's fortune-telling station has a line thirty people long. And it's just as well—because work will keep my mind off Daniel Carter Moon, the party pooper.

"Is it always like this on weekends?" Darcy asked Kevin as she brought in a Siamese cat for vaccinations.

"It's the last day of the fair, plus it's a Saturday, plus everyone is excited about the big dance party tonight," Kevin said. "Add that all together, and you get a whole new energy at the fair."

"I'll say," Darcy replied. "All the people waiting are actually smiling and being friendly. I was afraid they'd turn into an angry mob if we didn't move fast enough."

"Wouldn't *that* be exciting?" Kevin joked.

Lindsay took over assisting Kevin with the patients, and Darcy hung out at the counter, helping customers who wanted to buy pet food or other supplies. The commemorative doggy and kitty state-fair collars were a big seller.

In between customers, Darcy listened to the Great Jacktoni telling his bogus fortunes. Every time a new client sat down, Jack would study them for a moment before pulling out the tarot cards. When an older man sat down, Jack predicted that his retirement would be long and happy. When it was a teenage girl, he predicted that she'd be really popular in school next year. For a harried-looking father, he predicted that the kids would go to bed early that night.

Darcy had to hand it to him—he was getting pretty good at reading people. Although he still had no clue what any of the tarot cards meant.

"I can't believe he's really making money doing this," Lindsay said, coming up behind her.

"I know. When none of his predictions come true, all those people will think psychics are just frauds," Darcy said. "He's giving psychics a bad name!"

"Well, he's probably just doing what most psychics do," Lindsay said. "They usually find out about you by having an accomplice look at your driver's license or something, and then they figure out what to tell you based on that. It's all a bunch of psychological tricks."

Suddenly there was a stir among the customers for the Great Jacktoni. Everyone was whispering and looking toward the back of the line. "What's going on?" Lindsay asked.

A tall man in a long black robe stepped to the front of the line. He had thick salt-and-pepper hair swept back from his face and falling dramatically to his shoulders. His eyes were a light, piercing blue.

"Who is *that*?" Darcy asked.

"I am the Great Martoni," he boomed, turning to look right at her. Darcy gasped—she hadn't thought she said that loud enough for him to hear.

"Well, do you mind?" Jack asked, completely unfazed. "You're holding up my line."

Martoni peered down at him in silence for a moment.

Jack straightened his turban and looked right back.

"Are you the one who's stealing all my business today?" Martoni asked.

Jack shrugged. "It's not my fault if people want to pay less to hear their fortunes. My prices are simply more reasonable than yours."

"You are not a true psychic," Martoni said.

Jack stood up and crossed his arms. "Oh, yeah? Prove it."

Martoni's dark eyebrows shot up. "Prove it? How?"

"I challenge you to a duel," Jack said in a cocky voice. "A fortune-telling showdown!"

Everybody in the crowd gasped. Lindsay groaned. "Why does he have to be so arrogant all the time?" she said. "Now he's going to make a fool of himself."

"You never know," Darcy told her. "Maybe the Great Martoni is a fake, too."

"I accept your challenge," Martoni boomed. He turned and scanned the line of people. "We require a test subject." His gaze landed on Kevin, who had just come out of the examination room carrying a lop-eared rabbit. "You!" Martoni pointed to him.

Kevin stood still like a deer caught in the head-lights.

"You will be our guinea pig," Martoni said.

"Um, this is the Great Jacktoni's father," Darcy said. "It probably wouldn't be fair to use him."

"I'm not worried," Martoni assured her. "You. Sit."

Kevin handed the rabbit to Lindsay and sat down at Jack's fortune-telling table. "What's going on?" he whispered to Jack.

"Don't worry, Dad, I'm just gonna tell you your future," Jack said.

"It won't hurt, will it?" Kevin joked.

Jack shuffled the cards, making a big show of it. He looked like a professional card dealer. "My grandma taught him how to do that," Lindsay told Darcy. "She used to love to play Go Fish with us."

"Okay, pick seven cards," Jack said in his fake deep voice.

Kevin picked them. Jack laid them out on the table. He frowned and stroked his chin and even made a few "hmpff" noises. But the Great Martoni just watched with a slight smile on his face. He didn't look worried.

"I see it now," Jack said. "The pattern is becoming clear. You are going to give an animal a shot." He looked up triumphantly.

"Actually, no," Kevin said. "I just did my last vaccination of the day."

"Oh." Jack frowned. "I must have been seeing your past instead of your future. Let me look again." He stared at the cards.

"Nice recovery," Darcy murmured. Lindsay nodded.

"You will soon say good-bye to your son," Jack predicted. "You will use the proceeds from this week's state fair to send him on a monthlong trip to Hollywood!"

Kevin laughed. "I would've had to sell a lot of dog food to afford that. I'm afraid that's just wishful thinking, son. It's not my future—or yours."

"Darn," Jack muttered.

"I believe it's my turn," Martoni said. "May I?"

Reluctantly, Jack got up and gave his seat to the tall man. Martoni took the tarot cards, reshuffled them, and expertly laid them out before Kevin. As he worked, he said, "I'd like you to ask the cards a question—but don't tell me what it is."

"Okie-dokie," Kevin said.

Once the cards were on the table, Martoni glanced over them, nodding to himself. "All right." He looked up at Kevin. "The answer is yes."

"What?" Jack cried. "What's that supposed to mean? It could mean anything! You're not a psychic!"

Martoni kept his eyes on Kevin. "You used to dream of becoming a lounge singer," he said.

Jack burst out laughing. Even Darcy had to giggle at that one. Apparently the Great Martoni was just as big a fraud as Jack was.

"That's true. I did," Kevin said.

Jack fell silent. Lindsay's face paled. And Darcy's laughter died in her throat.

"What?" Lindsay croaked.

"It's the truth, honey. I've always wanted to be a singer," Kevin said. "I even have the perfect suit to wear for it—it's kind of shiny, and I'd wear it with a tie that had piano keys on it. I know what jokes I'd tell in between songs and everything."

"Am I dreaming?" Jack asked. "Is this a nightmare?"

Darcy tried to picture sensible, reliable Kevin in a shiny suit singing cheesy songs and telling jokes. She began to giggle again, but a look from Lindsay stopped her. "But wait, what was your question?" Darcy asked.

"He wondered if that dream would ever come true," Martoni answered for Kevin. "And the answer is yes. Tonight, in fact."

"That's amazing!" Kevin cried. "I'm signed up to start off the karaoke celebration at the dance tonight.

I didn't even tell my kids because I wanted it to be a surprise. How did you know about it?"

"He probably looked at the karaoke list," Jack said.

"No. Your father didn't use his real name," Martoni replied, studying the tarot cards. "I believe the name he used was I. Ken Tsing."

"I Can Sing?" Jack repeated.

"I thought it was funny," Kevin said. "It's a pun." He glanced at Lindsay. "Isn't it funny?"

"Are you really going to sing karaoke in front of everyone?" Lindsay asked.

Kevin nodded.

"Well, *that's* not funny," Lindsay said.

"Wait a minute," Darcy put in. "So you didn't tell anyone that you wanted to be a singer, or that you were going to sing tonight, or that you made up a silly stage name?"

"Not a soul," Kevin said.

"Then the Great Martoni really is a good fortune-teller!" Darcy cried.

"You're not kidding. I may just go back for another reading," Kevin said.

"Thank you." Martoni stood up. "Anyone who'd care to hear their true fortune is welcome to come with me to my booth." He walked off, his robe flowing majestically. And Jack's entire line of customers walked off with him.

"Thanks a lot, Dad," Jack muttered, pulling off his turban.

"Hey, at least you made some money," Darcy said.

"Only enough to pay for my turban," Jack said. He gave a dramatic sigh. "Oh, well, I'll just have to come up with some other scheme before next year's state fair."

"Darce, we have to go see Kathi and Skittles at the talent show," Lindsay said. "It's almost four thirty."

Darcy gasped. She'd been so busy watching Jack's fortune-teller showdown that she'd completely forgotten about the famous ballet-dancing pug!

"Do you need us any more today?" Darcy asked Kevin.

"Nope," he said. "You girls go do what you need to do."

Darcy shot Lindsay a smile. This was going to be fun!

The area around the center stage was packed with people. Everyone had brought picnic blankets and spread themselves out to have dinner and watch the talent show. It was a much bigger crowd than any of the girls had expected. Luckily, they had seats right in front of the stage because Skittles was a contestant.

"The stage looks really big," Kathi said nervously. She held Skittles in her arms and stared at the huge wooden structure.

"That's just because you're used to seeing it with a band on it, the way it's been all week," Darcy told her.

"All those amps and wires and music stands take up a lot of space."

"But Skittles is so small. Won't she get swallowed up by all that space?" Kathi stroked the pug's head. "She's already getting stage fright."

Skittles yawned.

"She'll be fine," Lindsay assured her. "They'll probably put a spotlight on her or something."

"Oh, no," Kathi moaned. "Skittles's eyes are very light-sensitive!"

"Shh," Darcy shushed them. "It's starting!"

Darcy had figured that the human portion of the talent show would come first, followed by the animal portion. But in fact, human acts and animal acts were all mixed together. The idea of people competing with animals for attention made her giggle. The prizes would be separate, but the audience's reaction would be the real test: Did people like to cheer on other people? Or would they root more for the cute little animals?

But when the first act came out, it was anything but a cute little animal. It was a huge emu, at least six feet tall, and it had a seriously bad attitude. The guy who owned the emu did a stand-up routine, telling lame jokes and using the emu as the straight man. Every time a joke hit the punch line, the emu would make a face or shake its whole body or bob its head in disgust. Once, it even pecked at the guy's butt, making him run in a circle while the emu chased him.

"I'm confused," Darcy whispered. "Whose talent are we watching, the bird's or the man's?"

"I think it's the man's," Lindsay whispered back. "But the bird is definitely more talented. Those jokes are awful!"

The next act was a girl on a unicycle. Somehow she managed to ride in figure eights, juggle three bowling pins, and yodel all at the same time.

"That's a lot of talent," Kathi said.

"I guess so," Darcy replied. "But I'm kind of scared she's going to ride right off the front of the stage!"

"You know who should be in this show?" Lindsay asked. "Daniel Carter Moon. He could demonstrate his talent of charming two girls at once."

Darcy giggled, but Kathi looked confused. "What?" she cried. "Wait. Daniel and Carter were dating two girls? *Wait*. Are you the two girls? Wait! Does that mean your dates for tonight are ruined?" Kathi spoke faster and faster, not even letting them get a word in. "Wait! He's a total jerk! What happened? What's going on?"

Lindsay smiled. "We'll tell you all about it after the talent show," she promised. "You need to concentrate on Skittles right now."

They watched a tap-dancing donkey, a fire-eating man, three really little kids who could seriously belt out show tunes, and a dog who howled the entire tune of "I Did It My Way."

Then Mikey and Alex came onstage.

"Hey, aren't those your friends from the surfing booth?" Kathi asked. "What are they doing here?"

"I don't know," Darcy said. "They never mentioned that they had entered the talent show."

"They're setting up some kind of . . . thing," Lindsay said, her brow furrowed in confusion.

Darcy looked at the stage. The twins each had a giant wooden frame with a smooth ramp in the shape of a quarter circle. Alex pushed his frame in from stage left, and Mikey pushed his in from stage right. "It's a half-pipe!" Darcy said with a grin. "For skateboarding."

"Aren't they champion skateboarders?" Kathi asked. "This is going to be cool!"

"I hope they win," Lindsay said. "They're the nicest guys."

Darcy studied her program as the brothers pushed the two halves of their half-pipe together into a full semicircular ramp. "It says here they're not competing," she read. "They're going to give a demonstration. They didn't think it would be fair to compete because they're already practically professional skateboarders."

"That's really cool of them," Lindsay said.

The half-pipe was ready, and the brothers took their positions on either side, poised at the top on their skateboards. Loud music blared from the speakers, and Mikey took off, flying down the pipe with his long hair streaming behind him. When he got to the top of the other side, Alex sped down into the pipe. Before long, they were doing jumps and twists and rolls, sometimes together and sometimes one at a time. Darcy had seen lots of skateboarding—it was hugely popular back in California. But even she didn't know the names of all the moves they pulled.

"This is awesome," she cried.

"No, it's *bodacious*," Lindsay replied. "That's what Alex and Mikey would say!"

When the twins had finished their show, everyone in the audience hooted and whistled. They were a huge hit!

Next came a pig who could balance plates on his snout and then a tall, thin man who kept trying to pull a rabbit out of his hat. Unfortunately, the rabbit kept hopping out on its own before it was supposed to. The rabbit got a lot of applause, but the magician mostly got laughed at.

Then it was Kathi's turn.

Darcy and Lindsay helped her up to the stage.
Kathi's face was completely white and her hands
shook. "Do you think Skittles is too nervous to go
on?" she asked.

Darcy glanced at the dog. She was licking up the
remains of a soda someone had spilled backstage.

"No, I think she'll be fine," Darcy replied. "And
so will you."

Kathi nodded, mustering up a smile. Lindsay
picked up Skittles, and Kathi slipped the rainbow
tutu over the pug's head, pulling it down to sit around
her middle. Darcy placed the sparkly tiara on her
head.

"Break a leg," she told Kathi.

Then the ballet music started, the spotlight went
on, and Kathi and Skittles headed out to center stage.

"All right, Skittles! You can do it, dog!" a voice
yelled from the front of the audience.

"Looking good, ballerina pug!" another voice
joined in.

Darcy peered into the crowd and spotted Mikey
and Alex, cheering and hollering for the pug. She
laughed as she saw them holding up their hands in a
surfers' hang-ten sign.

Kathi bowed. She said something to Skittles, and
the pug ran around in a little circle. The audience

laughed. Now it was time for the main event—Skittles's act of dancing around on her hind legs.

Kathi held a dog biscuit over the pug's head and gave her a command. She had a strange, haughty expression on her face.

"What is she doing?" Darcy whispered to Lindsay.

"She's pretending to be your mother in her queen-of-the-jungle movie," Lindsay explained. She looked at Darcy's surprised face. "Don't ask."

Skittles was gazing up at the dog biscuit as if she were hypnotized. But she made no move to dance on her hind legs.

Kathi's face grew even haughtier, and she gave the command again. But now Skittles was bored. She sat down in the center of the spotlight and swatted at the tiara, causing it to fall over one of her eyes.

The audience laughed.

Kathi reached for the tiara to fix it, but Skittles pulled away, making the tiara slip even farther down over her flat face. She grabbed it in her teeth and began playing tug-of-war with Kathi. The audience laughed even harder.

Finally Kathi managed to grab the tiara away from the pug. She held it up to examine it. But it didn't look like a tiara anymore—it looked more like a limp string of sequins.

"Uh-oh," Darcy said. "Maybe she should use it as a necklace."

"I don't think Skittles will go for that," Lindsay said. "Look!"

While Kathi was busy trying to get the tiara back into tiara-shape, Skittles had turned her attention to the tutu. She grabbed the brightly colored netting in her sharp little teeth and began to tug at it. But all that did was pull the tutu in a circle around her body. So Skittles began to chase it as it moved. Soon she was nothing but a blur of motion, racing around in tight little circles, rainbow-colored tulle flying in all directions as she tore it to shreds, all to the beautiful music from *Swan Lake*.

By this time, Kathi was in hysterics. But the audience was in stitches. When the music ended, Skittles stopped and looked around, confused. The audience roared. She got a standing ovation.

Kathi reached down and scooped her up, and Skittles barked in triumph all the way off the stage.

"Omigosh, that was horrible!" Kathi cried, running over to Darcy and Lindsay.

"No, it wasn't. It was hilarious," Darcy told her.

"But she didn't do anything right," Kathi wailed.

"It doesn't matter, Kathi," Lindsay said, leading her down the back steps of the stage. "The crowd loved it. You gave them all a big laugh."

"Yeah. They were laughing *at* me," Kathi said miserably.

"No. They were laughing at Skittles," Darcy corrected her. "Because she's a total clown. I mean, look at her. She loved it."

"Are you sure I didn't make a fool of myself?" Kathi asked as they made their way back to their seats.

"Absolutely," Darcy said.

"Positively," Lindsay added.

"Skittles!" Alex cried, rushing over to them. "You ruled!" He held out his hand. "Give me five, buddy."

Skittles slapped her paw into Alex's hand.

"That was totally off the charts," Mikey agreed. He plopped down onto their blanket. "I bet Skittles wins the whole animal contest."

"Well, I don't know about *that*," Darcy had to admit. "But she was definitely a crowd-pleaser."

But at the end of the show, the announcer gave out all the talent awards, then held up his hand for silence. "We have one more award," he called. "A very special one. It's for the Most Natural Performance. And it goes to a dog who's not afraid to be herself, even with a hundred people watching: Skittles Giraldi!"

The audience cheered as Kathi made her way up to

the stage to accept the award—a giant rawhide bone that was bigger than Skittles's whole body. Kathi was blushing furiously, but she also had a huge grin on her face.

"Looks like the talent show was a success after all," Darcy said to Lindsay.

Lindsay nodded. "Let's hope the rest of the night is a success, too," she said, looking at her watch. "We have to go get ready for the dance."

Darcy gasped. She'd been so wrapped up in watching the talent show that she'd almost forgotten about that jerk, Daniel Carter Moon. *Guess he wasn't as important as I thought he was,* she realized.

But that didn't stop her from wanting to teach him a lesson. It was time to put the get-Daniel-Carter-Moon plan into action!

Chapter 10

Wild Wisdom . . . *Scientists have discovered that chimpanzees use medicinal plants to treat themselves when they are ill or injured. This behavior is called "zoopharmacognosy."*

❋ DARCY'S DISH ❋

It's the moment of truth. The big dance is about to start, and our big plan is going to start right along with it! We're going to show Daniel Carter Moon that you don't mess with Darcy Fields and Lindsay Adams. At least I hope we are. Wish us luck!

"You guys look amazing!" Kathi cried, running up to Lindsay and Darcy. Kathi's hair was done in one long French braid, and she wore a pretty floral sundress.

"Thanks," Darcy said. "So do you."

"Darcy, did you see your mom?" Kathi rushed on. "She looks incredible. I mean, it's like the red carpet all over again. I bet she's wearing some designer dress, don't you think? Do you know where she got it?"

"Um . . . I haven't seen her yet," Darcy replied.

"Well, let's go," Kathi said. "She's over by the punch table. She's, like, completely mobbed by people. Jack is trying to act like her bodyguard, but nobody is paying any attention. But she's being really cool and signing autographs and everything. And we know her! It's so exciting!"

"Yeah, my mom is always friendly to her fans," Darcy said. "But Lindsay and I kinda have to take care of something before we can go hang out with her."

"Oh, right," Kathi said. She gave them a big wink. They'd explained their whole plan to her after the talent show. "Good luck. I'm gonna go hang out with your mom until the music starts. Maybe some reporter will take my picture with her!" She skipped off toward the punch table.

"We should find somewhere to hide," Lindsay said. "We don't want Carter to see us yet."

Darcy looked around. The big arena at the middle of the fairground was packed with people. The picnic blankets from the talent show audience were all cleared away, and a band was setting up on the wooden stage. Refreshment tables lined the edges of the space. "There aren't many places to hide," Darcy said.

"How about behind one of the big speakers?" Lindsay suggested. "From there we can see both sides of the dance floor."

They crept behind a tall speaker that stood on the ground next to the stage. Darcy checked her watch. "It's seven o'clock," she whispered.

"And there he is!" Lindsay said.

Sure enough, there was Daniel Carter Moon, weaving his way through the crowd. He wore a loose button-down shirt over a pair of perfectly broken-in jeans. *He's not cute; he's a jerk,* Darcy reminded herself. *Okay, well, he may be cute, but he's still a jerk,* she conceded.

Carter carried two huge sunflowers. He glanced around, as if he was afraid someone might see him. Then he quickly stashed one of the flowers in the pot of a ficus tree that was being used for decoration. He headed over to the north side of the dance floor with the other flower.

"I can't believe him! He brought the same flower for both of us," Darcy said.

"Shh. He's going to meet you," Lindsay said with a giggle.

Carter stood near the edge of the dance floor, looking around.

Lindsay pulled a walkie-talkie out of her purse. "Okay, Brett," she said into it. "The boy with the sunflower. Go!"

Darcy could see Brett Brennan at a table near the north side of the dance floor. He held a walkie-talkie, too. "Roger that," his voice crackled through the speaker.

Suddenly a chimpanzee went racing through the crowd. She wore Skittles's reworked tiara, big clip-on hoop earrings, and Darcy's striped and polka-dotted dress—cut down to chimp size. She loped right up to Carter and leapt into his arms.

Carter was so surprised that he dropped the sunflower. The chimp stretched one long arm down and snatched it back up. "What's going on?" Carter cried. He stared at the chimp for a moment and noticed the name tag stuck onto the front of her dress. It said: "Darcy."

Darcy the chimp gave him a big wet kiss on the cheek.

"Ugh!" Carter cried. He pried her arms from around his neck and put her on the ground while everyone around him laughed. Carter glanced at his watch, then took off toward the other side of the dance floor. Darcy the chimp ran after him, but he didn't notice.

Carter snatched the other sunflower from the ficus pot, straightened his shirt, and put on one of his killer smiles. He sauntered over to the south side of the dance floor.

"I can't believe him," Darcy cried. "He still thinks he's going to get a date with one of us!"

"Okay, Brandon, we're go on the south side," Lindsay said into the walkie-talkie.

"Gotcha," Brandon Brennan answered through the walkie-talkie. And suddenly another chimp was running toward Carter. This one wore a frilly pink party dress that Lindsay had been forced to wear for her birthday when she was eight. A matching pink bonnet completed the look.

The chimp jumped into Carter's arms and hugged him tight, blowing raspberries in his face. It didn't take Carter long to notice the name tag that said: "Lindsay."

His face fell. He tried to get Lindsay the chimp off of him, but she hung on. And Darcy the chimp finally caught up to him, too. She wrapped her arms around his legs and tried to dance with him.

Carter stumbled on to the dance floor, both chimps hugging and kissing him. People on all sides pointed and laughed.

Suddenly a burst of static filled the air. Then the bandleader's voice came over the big speakers. "Welcome to the State-Fair Dance," he boomed. "I see we've got one guy starting it off a little early tonight!"

On the dance floor, Carter's face turned red. Everyone else around the edges clapped and laughed.

"Looks like it's going to be a wild night!" the bandleader cracked. "Let's go!"

Music burst from the speakers and people streamed onto the floor, surrounding Carter and his dates.

Darcy and Lindsay were laughing so hard that they couldn't even speak. They high-fived each other, then waved at the Brennan brothers, who stood to either side of Carter, keeping a watch over their chimpanzees.

"Now *that* is the way to start a party," Darcy said.

"And the way to teach a two-timer his lesson," Lindsay added.

They looked at each other and laughed. "Now let's forget about Daniel Carter Moon and go have some serious fun," Darcy said.

"Luck be a lady toniiiiiight," Kevin belted out over the speakers. The karaoke machine played the music behind him, but he almost drowned it out with his loud voice.

171

"I can't believe I'm saying this, but he's not bad," Darcy said, and then took a sip of punch.

"I know. But he really should let someone else have a turn," Lindsay replied. "He's gotten up there every single time the band takes a break."

"Hey, he's living his dream," Darcy said, laughing. She turned in her seat to take in the scene. Her mother—looking gorgeous in the Versace dress she'd worn to the premiere of *Shooting Star*—was dancing with Brett, who was still dressed in overalls. Eli danced nearby with the Darcy chimp, who waved her arms around to the music.

Two tables away, Jack tried to teach the Lindsay chimp how to read tarot cards. She seemed more interested in playing with the turban she was now wearing. Every time Jack handed her the deck of cards, she threw them into the air and shrieked with amusement.

And right behind Jack and the chimp, heading straight toward their table, was Daniel Carter Moon!

"Yikes!" Darcy spun toward Lindsay. "It's Daniel! I mean Carter!"

Lindsay peered over her shoulder. "He's coming over here," she cried.

"What do we do?" Darcy asked.

Lindsay shrugged. "Tell him to go talk to the chimps?"

"Hi, Darcy. Lindsay," Carter said, stopping at their table.

"Um, hi, Daniel," Darcy said. "Or is it Carter? We got a little confused."

He winced. "I deserve that," he said.

"We didn't expect to see you again tonight," Lindsay said. "You know, once you finally managed to ditch the chimps."

"Yeah . . . what was that all about?" he asked.

"We just figured you deserved dates on the same level as yourself," Darcy said. "Although actually the chimps are pretty smart."

"And much nicer than you," Lindsay put in.

Carter looked down at his feet. "You're right. The chimps are probably better behaved than I was. I owe you guys an apology. As soon as I saw that you worked at the same booth, I should've realized you would figure it out."

Darcy couldn't believe him. "That is so not the point!" she cried. "You shouldn't have been dating us both in the first place. It doesn't matter whether we know each other or not."

"Yeah, you shouldn't be dating two girls at once, period." Lindsay frowned at him.

"Okay, okay, you're right," Carter said. "I'm sorry. I really am. But you got me back. I was totally embarrassed with the chimpanzee thing."

"Then we're even," Darcy said. "And we accept your apology."

"We do?" Lindsay asked. Darcy nodded. "Okay, I guess we do," Lindsay said.

"Just don't do this again when you move on to the next state fair," Darcy told him.

"I won't," Carter said. "I promise." He gave them one of his dimple-filled smiles. "So now that we're all friends again, do either of you want to dance?" he asked.

Darcy shook her head. "No thanks," she said. "We've already got partners."

"Oh." Carter looked confused. "Okay."

"See ya, Carter," Darcy said. Lindsay gave him a wave as he turned and headed off.

"He really is cute," Lindsay said.

"But it's much better to be with guys who are nice," Darcy replied.

Just then, Mikey and Alex came back to the table with two big plates full of food. "I figured we can share," Mikey said, slipping into the seat next to Darcy.

"Absolutely," she replied. "And then I want to dance some more."

"Me too," Lindsay said. She held up her cup of punch. "But first, a toast. To the fabulously successful new Simu-Surf business!"

"Um, actually, we made only enough money to cover the rental on our booth," Alex said. "Not enough to convince our mom that this is a super-amazing business idea."

"Yeah, but we did convince her to take us to California before the end of the summer," Mikey put in. "We're going to get to surf for real. On water!"

"Then here's to surfing on water," Lindsay said. They all clicked their plastic cups together.

"I have a toast, too," Darcy said. "I've never been to a state fair before, and I wasn't sure what to expect. But instead I had the greatest week ever. So here's to making new friends and helping each other have the best, most amazing, most totally bodacious state fair experience ever!"

They all toasted.

Darcy stood up, taking in the music and the crowd of people laughing and partying. "Now let's go have some more fun!"

The Many Troubles
of
Andy
Russell

Andy Russell's other (mis)adventures:

Andy and Tamika

**School Trouble
for Andy Russell**

**Parachuting Hamsters
and Andy Russell**

**Andy Russell,
NOT Wanted by the Police**

It's a Baby, Andy Russell

The Many Troubles
of
Andy
Russell

David A. Adler

With illustrations by
Will Hillenbrand

Gulliver Books
Harcourt, Inc.
Orlando Austin New York
San Diego Toronto London

For my son, Eddie,
and for his cousins, Shira and Dahlia

Thank you, Liz Van Doren,
for being my writing teacher, editor, and friend

For information about permission to reproduce selections from this
book, write to Permissions, Houghton Mifflin Harcourt Publishing
Company, 215 Park Avenue South, New York, New York 10003.

www.hmhco.com

First Gulliver Books paperback edition 1999

Gulliver Books is a trademark of Harcourt, Inc.,
registered in the United States of America and/or other jurisdictions.

The Library of Congress has cataloged an earlier edition as follows:
Adler, David A.
The many troubles of Andy Russell/David A. Adler;
with illustrations by Will Hillenbrand.
p. cm.
"Gulliver Books."
Summary: When some of his gerbils escape and he gets in trouble for not
paying attention in class, fourth-grader Andy Russell worries about asking
if a friend can move in with his family—especially when he learns that
his mother is going to have another baby.
[1. Family life—Fiction. 2. Friendship—Fiction. 3. Gerbils—Fiction.
4. Worry—Fiction.] I. Hillenbrand, Will, ill. II. Title.
PZ7.A2615Man 1998
[Fic]—dc21 98-10788
ISBN 0-15-201295-8
ISBN 0-15-205440-5 pb

Text set in Century Old Style
Designed by Kaelin Chappell
DOH 10 9 8 7
4500467304
Printed in the United States of America

Contents

Chapter 1
Gerbils on the Loose

Andy Russell rushed to the edge of the stairs and looked up. The doors to his parents' and sister Rachel's rooms were closed. He hurried back to the kitchen and climbed onto the counter by the sink. He reached up and pressed one hand to the ceiling to keep his balance.

Andy stretched. He was just able to touch the stack of plastic bowls on the top shelf of the cabinet, but he couldn't grab them.

I've got to stand on something else, Andy

thought. He looked down at the kitchen chairs. *Too high. If I put one on the counter and then stand on it, my head will hit the ceiling.* Andy looked at the shelf that held recipe cards and telephone books. *That's it,* he thought. *The Yellow Pages.*

Andy jumped from the counter. He opened the book to the back—1,288 pages. *That should do it.* Andy put it on the counter and climbed up.

He heard footsteps. He had to hurry. Someone was coming downstairs.

Andy pressed his hand against the ceiling again. He leaned forward and reached into the cabinet, but he still couldn't grab the bowls. He leaned forward a little more. Just as he got hold of the stack of bowls, his foot slipped and ripped the cover off the *Yellow Pages.* Andy fell into the sink. He knocked over a pot filled with soapy water and the bowls dropped from his hand to the floor.

The footsteps were getting closer.

Andy reached for the faucet to pull himself out of the sink, but his wet, soapy hand slipped and turned on the water. The water soaked the bottom of his pants legs and spilled on the floor.

"What happened? Are you hurt?" Mr. Russell

asked as he rushed into the kitchen and shut off the water.

"I'm just wet," Andy answered.

"Your foot is in the vegetable pot!" Mr. Russell said, and pulled a string bean off Andy's sneaker. "And your pants are all wet."

Andy held out his hand, and his father helped him out of the sink. "I was afraid Mom was coming down the stairs. I'm glad it was you."

"You didn't answer me. What happened? What were you doing in the sink? And take off those wet sneakers."

Andy took off his sneakers and socks. He collected the bowls while his father wiped the floor and counter with paper towels.

"Roll up the bottoms of your pants," Mr. Russell said. "They're dripping on the floor."

Andy rolled up his pants.

Mr. Russell wiped the floor again and asked, "Well, what were you doing in the sink?"

"I was getting bowls for the gerbils," Andy answered, "and I wouldn't have fallen into the sink and made such a mess if Mom didn't keep the bowls on the top shelf. Why does she do that?"

Andy looked up. His handprint was on the ceiling. All five fingers were nice and clear. He hoped his father wouldn't see it.

"Don't blame your mother for this mess," Mr. Russell said as he put the *Yellow Pages* back on the shelf. "She didn't fall in the sink. You did!"

Mr. Russell turned and looked at his son. "What happened to the bowls we bought at the pet shop?"

"They're still in the gerbil tanks, but believe me, Dad. We need more."

Mr. Russell refilled the vegetable pot with water and soap, and asked, "Why do we need more bowls?"

Just then Andy's older sister, Rachel, walked into the kitchen and said, "Hi, Monkey Face."

Rachel put a slice of bread into the toaster oven. She set the timer to two minutes and made sure to turn it and the toaster oven on at exactly the same moment.

Rachel ate the same breakfast every morning. "At two minutes, the toast is golden brown," she had once explained to her mother. "Anything more and it's too dark. Anything less and it's too bready."

"*Bready* is not a word," Mrs. Russell had told Rachel.

After two minutes, Rachel would put on a slice of American cheese and wait exactly one minute more, "So the cheese is just the right combination of soft and cheesy," Rachel had told her mother. "And *cheesy* IS a word!"

While Rachel stood by the toaster oven, she pointed at Andy's feet, held her nose, and said, "Wrap those in something. You're polluting the environment."

Andy made a face, pointed at his sister, and then spun one finger beside his head to indicate he thought she was crazy.

Rachel stuck out her tongue.

Then Andy whispered to his father, "Dad, come with me. I have to tell you something."

Andy took his socks and sneakers and led his father into the dining room.

"What is it?" Mr. Russell asked.

"It's trouble," Andy whispered. "Gerbil trouble. But I don't want Mom or Rachel to know about it. Please, promise you won't tell them."

Andy waited. His father didn't promise, but Andy was sure he would keep his secret. He was sure his dad wouldn't want Mrs. Russell or Rachel to know what he was about to tell him.

"I need the extra bowls"—Andy took a deep breath—"because I have to leave food in the basement and the hall because that's where some of them are."

"What!" Mr. Russell shouted.

"Sh!" Andy whispered.

He tiptoed to the doorway to see if Rachel had heard his father scream. She had one hand ready to open the toaster-oven door. She was watching the timer. Andy tiptoed back to his father. He was still holding his socks and sneakers.

"The gerbils in the middle tank got out," Andy whispered, "and I don't know how that happened unless, maybe, they watched me open and close it so often that they learned how to do it themselves. If I don't leave food for them, they might starve."

Andy suspected he hadn't completely closed the screen on top of the gerbils' tank, and he was sure his father suspected the very same thing. He was just glad his father didn't seem really angry.

"How many gerbils are out?" Mr. Russell asked.

"Well," Andy replied, "I think maybe seven. But don't worry. I'll take care of them. They're mostly in the basement, but I saw one in the upstairs hall, so that's where I'm leaving the food."

As Mr. Russell hurried to the basement, he told Andy, "I'm not worried about the gerbils. I'm worried about the house and your mother. She hasn't been feeling well, and I'm sure something like this would really upset her."

Andy was also sure it would upset her. His mother didn't like animals. She only agreed to let Andy have pets when he assured her she wouldn't have to take care of them, and if she didn't go into the basement, she wouldn't even see them.

Mr. Russell opened the door to the basement. He and Andy went in. Then Mr. Russell quickly closed the door.

From the top of the stairs, Andy looked around the large room. Along the wall with the staircase was a row of low bookcases, each with three shelves filled with books, toys, and the blocks Andy played with when he was much younger. On top of the bookcases were four tanks, three for his gerbils and one for his pet snake, Slither. Along the next wall hung framed family photographs. In front of the remaining two walls were a couch, a small table, and chairs.

Ta. Ta. Ta.... Ta. Ta. Ta.

"I think there's one under the couch," Andy said.

"Catch it! Catch it!" Mr. Russell told him.

They quickly ran down the steps. Mr. Russell lifted the front end of the couch. It was heavy. Inside, it had a hidden bed.

The gerbil looked up at Mr. Russell.

Andy gently put down his socks and sneakers. He walked very slowly toward the gerbil. "Don't be afraid," Andy said softly.

"I'm *not* afraid," Mr. Russell told him. "I'm upset, and I can't hold this up much longer."

"Dad, I was talking to the gerbil."

Andy moved slowly. "Don't be afraid," he said again. "I'm going to put you back in your home, where there's plenty of food and water and toys. I'm your friend, so don't be afraid."

"Don't sweet-talk him," Mr. Russell said. "Just catch him! Catch him!"

Andy reached for the gerbil's tail, but before he could catch it, the gerbil ran behind the bookcase. Mr. Russell slowly lowered the couch, and when it was just a few inches above the floor, he let it drop.

Bam.

Suddenly the basement door opened and Mrs. Russell looked in. "What are you doing down there? This is a school day. The bus will be here soon."

Mrs. Russell looked at Andy. She shook her head slightly and added, "Roll down your pants legs and put on your socks and sneakers."

"Yes, Mom."

"Please close the door," Mr. Russell said.

"Whatever you're doing down there, do it fast," Mrs. Russell told him. "Andy can't miss the bus, and Charles, you can't be late for work, especially not now." Then she closed the door.

"Why can't you be late for work, Dad?"

"Let's just catch the gerbils," Mr. Russell answered. It was clear to Andy that his father didn't want to say why he had to be on time. *Maybe Dad's in trouble at work,* Andy thought. *Maybe he messed up.*

"I'll catch them all, Dad. I promise."

Ta. Ta. Ta. . . . Ta. Ta. Ta.

A gerbil was running under the baseboard

heater. Andy reached for its tail, but the gerbil ran behind a bookcase and Andy couldn't get it.

"Dad, please, don't tell Mom they got out. She doesn't like my pets, and if she finds out the gerbils are loose, she won't, well, she won't be happy."

An odd look came over Mr. Russell's face and then the hint of a smile. He spoke slowly. "Gerbils on the loose will upset Mom, and we don't want that. If Mom doesn't ask me about them, I won't mention it."

Crash!

A gerbil had knocked over an open box of plastic stacking clowns and spilled them across the basement floor. Andy lunged after the gerbil and landed on the clowns. "Ouch!" Andy exclaimed as he reached under his stomach, pulled out a clown, and tossed it into the box. Then he sat up and put the other clowns in the box, too.

"Don't worry so much about me telling Mom," Mr. Russell said. "Worry about the gerbils. If they're not careful and keep knocking things over, I won't have to tell her they're loose. She'll find out on her own."

Chapter 2
Slither the Snake

Before Andy and his father went upstairs, they checked the screen tops of the two other gerbil tanks. The gerbils were inside, playing on the exercise wheels, crawling through the tunnels, and chewing the colored construction paper Andy had left for them the night before. The gerbils had chewed most of the paper into tiny pieces.

"They're busy making confetti," Andy told his father.

Andy sometimes called the gerbil tanks "confetti factories." The shelves of his closet were filled with bags of gerbil-made confetti. Andy was saving them to sell for New Year's Eve.

Mr. Russell was proud of Andy's confetti project. He said it showed Andy had a "real head for business," that when he finished school he would be able to take care of himself. Mrs. Russell wasn't impressed. She said, "If I find one scrap of gerbil-chewed paper upstairs, those animals go back to the pet shop!"

Next, Andy and his father looked in Slither's tank. The snake was Andy's reward for six "Be Good" weeks at the end of third grade, when he had paid attention in class and didn't argue with his teacher, Mr. Hoover. Andy had hoped to get a poisonous cobra or a squeezing python, but his parents refused to buy a dangerous snake and bought Slither instead, a nonpoisonous, nonsqueezing garter snake.

Slither ate minnows. Andy liked to watch the small bulge move down Slither's skinny body as he slowly digested each fish.

A few days after Andy got the snake, Slither escaped and was gone for three weeks. Mr.

Russell was sure he had slithered out of the house. He felt bad for Andy and bought two gerbils to take the snake's place. Andy put them in Slither's tank.

Mr. Russell had asked Jeff at the pet shop for male gerbils. It was clear a few weeks later, when Andy discovered one of the gerbils nursing seven babies, that Jeff had made a mistake. A while later she had babies again. Later the babies had babies.

And Slither hadn't slithered out of the house.

A few days after Andy got the gerbils, it rained. Rachel put her foot in her left rain boot and screamed.

She had found Slither.

Andy thanked Rachel for finding his snake, but she was screaming too loud to hear him. Rachel hated Andy's pets, perhaps even more than their mother did.

By this time the gerbils were living in Slither's tank, so Andy emptied an apple-juice jar, then put in some dirt, leaves, and Slither. Andy's father poked a few small holes in the top of the jar so the snake could breathe. That afternoon Mr. Russell bought a new tank with a screen on top.

Andy smiled now as he looked at Slither. The snake turned his head toward Andy. Slither stuck out his forked tongue. The tongue darted in and out a few times.

Andy said, "Good morning, Slither," and stuck out *his* tongue.

Andy checked his socks and sneakers. They were still wet. He hid them behind a chair and followed his father upstairs. Rachel was standing by the front door. "You'd better hurry," she told Andy as she left the house.

Andy ran upstairs, rolled down his pants legs, got dry socks, and put them on. Then he put on his dry winter boots. He ate a quick breakfast— a granola bar and chocolate milk.

Mrs. Russell stood by the door and watched Andy put on his jacket, take his backpack and lunch bag, and open the front door. Before she could ask him why he was wearing boots in the fall, Andy told his mother, "You look lovely this morning."

"Thank you," Mrs. Russell said as she went to the closet to get her own coat.

Andy was proud of himself. He had distracted his mother and said just the right thing. He thought that now, if she saw a gerbil on the couch, she might remember that he had said she looked lovely and not get so angry.

Andy ran to the bus stop and waited there with Rachel and the Belmont girls. He looked at Rachel and remembered when she had found Slither. She had run upstairs, changed her socks, washed her feet, and screamed again and again about "that slimy, stinky thing."

"Snakes don't stink!" Andy had told Rachel as he gently took Slither out of her boot.

Andy smiled as he wondered what Rachel would do if she found gerbils in her boots. She'd probably scream so loud she would get laryngitis. Then she wouldn't be able to talk. *A quiet Rachel!* Andy thought that would be great.

Andy's parents drove past the bus stop. Mrs. Russell was driving. First she would leave Mr. Russell off at the library, where he was helping to build an extension to the reading room. He was a carpenter and was doing some of the woodwork. Then Mrs. Russell would go to the high school, where she taught mathematics.

Just as Andy saw the bus approaching, he realized he had forgotten to leave out the bowls of food. The house was locked and his parents were gone. Rachel had a key, but to get it, he would have to tell her about the gerbils. And, even with the key, if he ran home, he would miss the bus and have no way to get to school. Andy realized there was nothing he could do. He had real trouble this morning. He hoped the gerbils wouldn't be hungry and that he could catch them all before his mother or Rachel discovered they were out.

The bus stopped and the door opened. Rachel and the Belmonts got on, and just as Andy put his right foot on the first step, Tamika Anderson shouted, "Wait! Wait for me!"

Andy waited for Tamika with his right foot on the first step of the bus and his left foot on the curb.

"You can get on. I'll wait for her," Mr. Cole, the bus driver, said. "Don't I always wait for her?"

It was true. Tamika was late for the bus almost every morning, and when she yelled, "Wait!" Mr. Cole always did.

Andy got on the bus and said hello to his friend Bruce, who was sitting near Mr. Cole.

Bruce put one hand on his head and the other beneath his chin. Then he waved both hands. A long time ago, when they had first met at school, Andy had made that their secret wave. But now he wished Bruce would not do that every morning. He thought a secret wave was kindergarten stuff.

There were no empty seats near Bruce. Andy found one in the back, right behind Rachel. Tamika followed him onto the bus. Her sneakers were untied and her shirtsleeves were unbuttoned.

"I'm sorry I made you wait," she told Mr. Cole. She stood for a moment just inside the bus, trying to catch her breath.

"That's OK," the bus driver said as he pulled the lever to close the door. "I'm used to it."

Tamika walked down the narrow aisle and took the seat across from Andy.

"Hi," Andy said.

"Hi," Tamika replied. "I was helping Mrs. Perlman wash the breakfast dishes. That's why I'm late."

Andy held Tamika's backpack while she tied her shoes and buttoned her shirtsleeves. She took a mirror from her pack and looked into it.

"Yuck!" she said. "My hair ribbons don't match my shirt."

"And your socks don't match each other," Andy said as he returned her backpack. "One's red and the other is brown."

"I'll get up earlier tomorrow. I will."

"Maybe," Andy said. "Or maybe you'll be late again and say what you always say, that you'll get up earlier tomorrow."

Tamika took a deep breath and then asked, "Did you talk to your parents yet?"

Andy shook his head and pointed to Rachel. Tamika didn't understand.

Andy took out his homework pad. He opened to a blank page and wrote, I DIDN'T ASK MY PARENTS YET AND RACHEL DOESN'T KNOW ABOUT IT!

"We can tell Ra—," Tamika started to say, but Andy put his finger to his lips and gave Tamika the homework pad. Tamika wrote, WE CAN TELL RACHEL. SHE'S MY FRIEND, TOO.

Andy took back the pad and read Tamika's message. Then he shook his head and wrote, I'LL TAKE CARE OF THIS.

He gave Tamika the pad. She turned to the

previous page and asked, "Did we have any history homework?"

"We had to review chapter seven."

"We did?" Tamika asked. She looked out the bus window. "We're at Hamilton Avenue. I have time," she said, and took out her history book.

When they arrived at school, the yard was already clear. Tamika and Andy were the last off the bus. They hurried into the building.

All during class Andy looked right at Ms. Roman, his fourth-grade teacher. He didn't want her to think he wasn't listening. Then she might write another note to his parents. But he *wasn't* listening. He was thinking about the gerbils, wondering if they were still in the basement, if they were hungry, and if his mother would go home for lunch and find them. Andy imagined the gerbils outside their tank, looking in, seeing the food, water, toys, and paper, and feeling sorry they had left their comfortable home. He was also thinking about his secret with Tamika.

"Andrew, are you paying attention?" Ms. Roman asked.

Andrew was Andy's real name. But only Ms. Roman called him that.

Andy considered changing the subject by telling Ms. Roman she looked lovely. But then he looked at her big gray tent dress and brown work shoes, and decided that even Ms. Roman wouldn't believe she looked good.

"Andrew, are you paying attention?" Ms. Roman asked again.

Andy smiled. "Yes, Ms. Roman."

"Then what's the answer?"

The answer? What was the question?

Andy looked at Tamika, and she shook her head. She hadn't been listening, either.

Andy looked next at his friend Bruce. He was busy scribbling in his notebook. Andy thought Bruce was probably writing another silly poem.

Ms. Roman was standing next to the globe. Perhaps she had asked Andy a geography question. He remembered that China is the name of a country where a lot of people live and that dishes are made of it, and he thought it could be the answer to lots of questions.

"China," Andy said.

"China! What sort of an answer is that? We're doing math!"

A few of Andy's classmates laughed. Many of

the others looked up. It was clear to Andy that they weren't paying attention, either. They hadn't heard Ms. Roman's question nor Andy's ridiculous answer.

Ms. Roman called on Stacy Ann Jackson. Stacy Ann sat right in front of Andy.

"Four hundred and twelve," Stacy Ann said in her best I-know-and-you-don't tone.

"That's right."

"Thank you," Stacy Ann said sweetly to Ms. Roman. Then, when Ms. Roman turned to the chalkboard, Stacy Ann whispered to Andy, "*I* was listening."

Andy hated Stacy Ann Jackson. She was so phony. He couldn't understand why Ms. Roman and all the other teachers liked her.

Andy tried to pay attention to the rest of the math lesson, but it was a real struggle. He kept thinking about the gerbils and his secret with Tamika. Andy was relieved when the bell rang and it was time for lunch.

In the cafeteria, Andy, Tamika, and Bruce sat far away from most of their classmates. Andy was about to tell Tamika and Bruce about the gerbils when Bruce took a paper from his shirt pocket

and asked, "Do you want to hear the poem I wrote during math?"

"No."

Bruce read it anyway.

"A crocodile bath
or doing math.
Which is worse?
Ask the nurse."

"Very nice," Andy said. "Now eat your lunch."

"I'm calling this poem 'Crocodile Math,' and I'm going to submit it to the school newspaper or maybe to a magazine."

"Why would you ask a nurse about a crocodile or math?" Tamika asked. "She knows about Band-Aids and thermometers, not reptiles and numbers."

"I was using my creative license," Bruce answered as he carefully folded the paper and returned it to his shirt pocket. "My dad says I'm creative, and creative people make a difference. We change the world."

Andy said, "I hope creative people change their underwear, too."

"What!"

"Just kidding! Eat your lunch," Andy said again, "so I can tell you about my gerbil troubles."

Bruce opened his lunch bag and unwrapped the aluminum foil from his sandwich. He lifted the corner of the top slice of bread and said, "Cream cheese again! I get the same boring lunch every day."

Andy gave his sandwich to Bruce.

Bruce inspected Andy's sandwich and said, "Ah, peanut butter."

Bruce offered to trade Andy his cream-cheese sandwich, but Andy didn't want it. "I can't eat. I have too many troubles."

Andy gave Bruce his apple and cupcake, too. He opened his container of chocolate milk, pushed in a straw, and drank slowly.

"Hey, thanks," Bruce said.

He took the tops off the two sandwiches and turned the two slices of bread and cream cheese over, placing them on top of the two halves of Andy's sandwich. "Now I have two cream-cheese-and-peanut-butter sandwiches."

Bruce remade the sandwiches. After he bit into one, Tamika said, "You didn't have to put them together. If you ate them separately, you would have been eating the same thing. Everything just gets mixed up in your stomach anyway."

"Ig taks etter is ay," Bruce said with his mouth full of cream cheese, peanut butter, and bread. He swallowed and said again, "It tastes better this way."

"Oh, stop talking about food. I have real important stuff to tell you," Andy said. "But not here. Outside."

"As soon as I finish," Bruce said.

Tamika ate her lunch quickly, threw out her empty bag, and waited with Andy while Bruce ate the sandwiches, an orange, and Andy's apple and cupcake. He drank two containers of apple juice.

"Are you done?" Andy asked.

Bruce checked inside his lunch bag and Andy's to see if there was anything left. There wasn't.

"Done," he said. "Let's go outside."

Bruce dropped the aluminum foil, empty lunch bags, and drink containers in the large garbage can by the door. Then Andy led Tamika and Bruce outside.

"Hey, Tamika!" Rachel called. She was jumping

rope with a group of her friends. "Do you want to play?"

Tamika shook her head and pointed to Andy.

Andy led Tamika and Bruce to a corner of the playground and told them about the gerbils.

"So why is that such a big secret?" Bruce asked.

Andy pointed to Rachel. "We have to catch the gerbils before my mother or Rachel finds out. Will you help?"

"I really want to," Tamika said, "but I can't. I have to go to the dentist. The Perlmans want my teeth checked before they go to South America."

The Perlmans were Tamika's foster parents. She had been living with them for the past year, ever since Tamika's parents were badly hurt in a car accident. At first it was expected this arrangement would last just a few months, but the Andersons were still in a rehabilitation center, and now the Perlmans were preparing to go to South America for their work.

"I'll help," Bruce said. "It will be fun. We can pretend we're on a lion safari. No...no, a gerbil safari."

The bell rang. Lunch period was over. Bruce ran toward the door. Andy was about to follow him when Tamika grabbed his arm. "When will you ask your parents if I can move in?" Tamika asked. "Please, do you think you can ask them today?"

That was Andy's secret with Tamika. He had promised to ask his parents if she could stay with his family for the year the Perlmans would be in South America—or until her parents were better.

"I'll talk to them. I promise. And if they say yes, they'll speak to Rachel. They'll probably want you to stay in her room and, believe me, it's better for my parents to ask Rachel instead of you or me."

Tamika said, "Maybe you're right."

"But first," Andy told her, "I have to get all the gerbils. If Mom finds one upstairs, she might not even let *me* stay in the house."

After lunch Ms. Roman talked about the fourth-grade carnival. It would raise money for charity and would be in three weeks, on the Monday before Thanksgiving. She wanted everyone to think of fun booths and to look at home for books and toys they no longer wanted. They would use them as prizes. The money they raised would be for the local soup kitchen to help pay for their Thanksgiving dinner. Andy thought making a carnival would be exciting. But even though he tried to listen to the talk about the booths and the prizes, he kept thinking about the gerbils.

When the school bell rang, Ms. Roman looked out across the class, smiled, and said, "Well, that's it. You go home and do your homework, and I'll prepare tomorrow's lessons. Go on."

School was out.

Andy loaded his backpack. He didn't want to think about which books he needed for homework, so he took them all.

Stacy Ann Jackson turned.

She smiled.

Then she took a note from her pocket. FOR ANDY was written on the outside of it. It was from Bruce. Stacy read from the note. "Should I bring my butterfly net? It might help us catch the gerbils."

Stacy Ann wrinkled her nose. She bent her fingers so her hands looked like paws and held them near her face. "Did your gerbils get out?" she squeaked.

"That was *my* note," Andy said, and grabbed it.

Stacy Ann smiled. "It landed by my desk. I thought it was for me."

Stacy Ann picked up her books. "Rachel must love having wild, stupid rodents running through your house. It's almost as bad as having a wild, stupid brother."

Stacy Ann Jackson turned and left the room.

Andy grabbed his backpack and started to run after her, but he had grabbed his pack upside down and all his books and papers fell out.

"Tamika, Bruce!" Andy called. "Stop her! Stop Stacy Ann! Don't let her talk to Rachel."

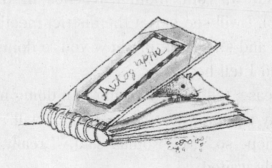

Chapter 3
More Trouble

Tamika and Bruce ran out of the room.

Andy packed his backpack again and this time he closed the zipper. He hurried toward the door, but before he could leave the room, Ms. Roman stopped him.

"Andrew, I was disappointed this morning. You weren't paying attention to the math lesson."

Ms. Roman was sitting at her desk. The class record book was open.

"I can't really talk now," Andy said. "If I don't hurry outside, I'll miss my bus."

"Andrew, your mother teaches in the high school. I will see her at the district meeting next week and she'll ask me how you're doing. What should I tell her?"

"Please, tell her I'm trying. I'm doing my best. I'll pay attention tomorrow. I really will."

"I hope so," Ms. Roman said. "I really do."

Andy waited.

"That's it," Ms. Roman said. "Now you hurry to the bus."

Andy ran outside and found Tamika and Bruce standing right in front of Stacy Ann. When she moved one way, so did they. When she moved the other way, they did, too.

"Let me go," Stacy Ann shouted. "I'll miss my bus."

Andy looked at the buses waiting by the curb. Some already had their engines running. "Let her go," Andy said. He couldn't worry about Stacy Ann Jackson now. He was too upset by the prospect of Ms. Roman telling his mother that he answered "China" to a *math* problem. His mother taught math and thought it was *so* interesting.

Stacy Ann ran to her bus. It was the first in line. She got on just before the door closed. Andy, Tamika, and Bruce went to their bus.

Rachel was sitting right behind Mr. Cole. "Hi, Monkey Face," she said when Andy got on.

"Yeah, sure," he answered.

Andy, Tamika, and Bruce sat together on the last seat. "I told Stacy Ann her slip was showing," Tamika said. "That's how I got her to stop. Then she looked down and saw that she wasn't wearing a dress or slip. She was wearing pants. Isn't that great!"

Andy nodded.

Bruce said, "And I told her she had her socks on the wrong feet. You see, Stacy Ann is not always so smart. Sometimes *I'm* the smart one. It doesn't matter what foot you put your socks on."

Andy turned to Bruce and said, "Well, smart one, it was because of your note about the butterfly net that Stacy Ann knows about the gerbils. Writing that note and throwing it near her desk wasn't very smart. And, as if your note and the gerbils aren't enough trouble, Ms. Roman reminded me that she's going to see my mom at a meeting next week. If I don't start paying attention, I know she'll tell my mother."

Andy looked out the window and said softly, "And it's so hard to listen in her class."

The bus started to move. Andy turned from the window and was startled to see Bruce staring at him.

"I'm sorry about the note," Bruce said, "and I'm sorry about Ms. Roman." He waited a moment. Then he looked down at the floor of the bus and asked softly, "Can we still play gerbil safari?"

"Sure," Andy replied. "I'll give you a big hunter's gun that shoots tranquilizer pellets."

"Really?"

"Of course not. I'm just kidding."

"And Andy," Tamika said, "don't worry so much about Ms. Roman. When she meets your mother, she'll probably tell her something good."

"Yeah," Bruce said. "Sometimes I worry so much about something, then it never happens."

During the ride home, while Tamika and Bruce talked, Andy stared out the window. He knew Tamika and Bruce were probably right, but still, he worried.

Andy imagined Ms. Roman telling his mother, "Your son Andrew pays absolutely no attention in class. It's a wonder he learns anything! One day he'll wake up from whatever he dreams about and find the school day is over and everyone has gone home."

Why does Mom have to be a teacher? Andy asked himself. *Why can't she be a carpenter, like Dad. He never meets Ms. Roman at meetings.* Then Andy remembered the gerbils. He hoped his mother hadn't gone home for lunch and found them running around the house.

"Let's go! Let's go! It's our stop," Tamika said. She was shaking Andy.

Andy, Tamika, and Bruce ran down the center aisle of the bus and jumped down the two steps to the street.

"I'll see you tomorrow," Tamika said after they had crossed the street. "And please, ask your parents about me." She ran next door to the Perlmans'.

"What did she say about your parents?" Bruce asked.

Andy turned, looked at Bruce, and said, "I can't tell you right now."

"You're keeping a secret from me?" Bruce asked. "But I'm your best friend."

"I really can't tell you," Andy said again. "I really can't."

Andy walked ahead. When he reached his house, Rachel was already there, opening the front door. Andy pushed in ahead of her and said, "Bruce and I are working in the basement, so stay out!"

"Don't worry. You can go in that basement with the gerbils and snake. I do my homework in the kitchen."

Andy stuck out his tongue at Rachel. Bruce smiled. Then they both hurried to the basement and closed the door.

Bruce sat at the end of the couch, next to the small table with the telephone. He picked up the handset and punched in his number. When his mother answered, he said, "I'm at Andy's. Can I stay to play and do my homework?" He listened and said, "Thanks, Mom."

After Bruce hung up the telephone, he and Andy searched the basement for gerbils.

The box of plastic stacking clowns had been

turned over again. There was lots of chewed-up paper on the floor.

Ta. Ta. Ta. . . . Ta. Ta. Ta.

"Sh. There's one under the heater," Andy whispered.

Andy took off his backpack and walked slowly toward the baseboard heater. Bruce followed him.

A gerbil tail was sticking out from under the heater.

Andy reached for the gerbil, but it ran toward Bruce with its tail still sticking out. Bruce took out his pocket ruler and stuck it under the heater, blocking the way. The gerbil stopped, turned, and ran back to where Andy was waiting. He grabbed its tail, pulled the gerbil out, and as he carried it to the tank, he told the gerbil, "I was worried about you. I'm glad you didn't starve."

"That was great," Andy told Bruce. "You're the chaser. I'm the catcher. We're a team."

"Yeah," Bruce said. "You don't have to worry. We'll catch all the gerbils."

Andy and Bruce searched for more gerbils. When they didn't find any, Andy put his ear flat on the floor and listened for them.

"There's something under there," Andy said, and crawled to the big cloth-covered chair. He reached under it and took out an autograph book. Andy said, "It's Rachel's. She's been searching all over for this."

He flipped through the book. "The gerbils chewed some of the pages—through Donna's poem, Beth's rebuses, and Freddy's icky birthday note. Now I'm in more trouble."

He put the book in his back pocket.

Andy found gerbil teeth marks in the television wire, too, and in the bottom of the bookcase.

"Your gerbils are worse than termites," Bruce said. "They must be really hungry."

For the next hour, Andy and Bruce listened, searched for, and chased after gerbils. Andy caught one more by grabbing its tail and another by dropping a towel on top of it; he scooped up the towel and put the gerbil gently into the tank.

"Maybe that's all of them," Bruce said.

"No. There were at least seven."

Click.

Bruce said, "I think I hear something."

"Uh-oh. That's not a gerbil," Andy told him. He quietly climbed the basement stairs and pushed

open the door just a little. "It's my parents," Andy whispered. "They're home early."

Through the crack in the open door, Andy watched his mother come in first. She moved very slowly, hardly lifting her feet. Her coat was hanging open with the belt dragging on the floor. Mr. Russell was right behind her. He helped her into the house.

Andy whispered to Bruce, "They're home early. I wonder what's wrong." Andy watched his parents go upstairs and then said, "Mom looks sick."

Bruce said, "I bet your dad told her about the gerbils. That's why she's sick."

"Oh, I hope not," Andy said. "He promised he wouldn't."

Andy waited. He expected someone to scream for him to come upstairs. When no one did, he told Bruce, "I may as well get it over with."

Bruce said, "Don't worry. Your mom knows you're just a kid."

"I don't think that will help," Andy said. He took a deep breath and told Bruce, "You stay here and look for gerbils. I'll go upstairs so Mom can yell at me."

Chapter 4
The Secret

A ndy wondered what his mother would say and what he could tell her. *I know,* he thought. *I'll tell her not to yell at me. She should yell at the gerbils. They're the ones running loose and leaving droppings all over the house.* Then Andy thought, *Maybe I shouldn't say anything about the droppings.*

Andy walked past the kitchen. Rachel was sitting at the table with her schoolbooks in a neat pile on her left and one book open in front of her. To her right was a glass of milk on a place mat along with a neatly folded napkin.

You're lucky, Andy thought. *You never get in trouble.*

Andy thought some more about what he could tell his mother. *I know. I'll promise to punish the gerbils. I'll take away their toys and when the TV is on, I'll cover their tank with a dark cloth so they can't watch.* Andy smiled. *That's pretty funny.*

Andy walked upstairs, to his parents' bedroom. Mrs. Russell was lying on the bed with her eyes closed. She was still dressed in her school clothes. Even her shoes were still on. Mr. Russell was sitting beside her, holding a large green basin.

"Hello, Mom."

Mrs. Russell opened her eyes. She slowly lifted her head and looked at Andy. Her eyes were red. Her lips were pale. Her skin was almost green.

"Mom, you look terrible."

Mrs. Russell put her head down.

"I'm sorry you feel so bad and I know it's my fault. But don't worry. Bruce and I caught three of them. I'll go right back down and catch the rest."

"That's nice," Mrs. Russell said with her head still on the pillow. "You have a nice catch with Bruce."

Mr. Russell put the basin down and got up from the bed. He took Andy's arm and led him out of the room. "Your mother is not feeling well," he whispered.

"It's your fault, Dad. You shouldn't have told her about the gerbils."

Mr. Russell put his finger to his lips and said, "Sh, she doesn't know about the gerbils and don't you tell her."

"Then why does she look like that? Is she sick?"

"No."

Andy looked in the room. Mrs. Russell was leaning over the basin.

"She sure *looks* sick," Andy said. "She's about to barf."

"Go into your room and wait there," Mr. Russell told him. "I'll get Rachel. I need to talk to both of you."

Andy wondered what his dad needed to talk about. *Maybe Mom had caught that "berry-berry" disease from the gerbils, or some rare Chinese virus. Maybe the house will be quarantined. That wouldn't be so bad. I'll probably learn more watching cartoons all day than listening to Ms. Roman.*

When Andy sat on the edge of his bed, he felt Rachel's autograph book in his pocket. He pushed the book in deeper, so it wouldn't stick out. Then he scooted back, stretching his legs out on top of the bed. If his mother could wear her shoes in bed, then so could he.

Bruce walked into the room. "Hey! Look what I caught!" He was holding a gerbil by its tail. The gerbil was wriggling, trying to get loose.

Andy jumped off his bed. "Get downstairs with that and don't let anyone see you. I don't need more trouble."

Andy peeked into the hall and saw his father and Rachel coming up the stairs. They stopped to look in on Mrs. Russell.

"No. Don't go to the basement. Hide."

"Where?" Bruce asked.

Andy looked around the room.

"In my closet. No. It's full of stuff. There's no room. Hide under the bed."

Bruce quickly crawled under the bed. Andy draped a blanket over the side and sat down.

"Quit wriggling," Bruce said.

Andy bent forward and told him, "I'm not wriggling."

"Not you. The gerbil. It's getting loose."

"Hey, Monkey Face," Rachel said as she walked in. She looked for someplace to sit. "What a mess," she said as she pushed books, papers, candy wrappers, and a pair of pajamas off Andy's desk chair and sat down.

Mr. Russell leaned against the edge of Andy's desk. He started to say something and then stopped.

"It's not my fault," Andy said quickly. "The man at the pet shop didn't say anything about a berry disease or a virus from gerbils."

Mr. Russell looked at his son. "Andy, what I'm about to tell you has nothing to do with gerbils."

"Then it's Ms. Roman," Andy said. "It's impossible to listen to her all the time. She's as boring as breadsticks."

"As boring as breadsticks?" Rachel asked. "What does that mean?"

"Stop it, both of you," Mr. Russell said. A strange look came over his face and then a faint smile. "I have something important and wonderful to tell you," he said, "but it's a secret, a good secret."

"A *good* secret?" Rachel asked.

"Did we win the lottery?" Andy asked.

"It's better than the lottery," Mr. Russell said. "It's the best secret there is."

Mr. Russell smiled again.

"Your mother isn't sick."

He paused.

"And she really doesn't want people at her school making a fuss, so she's not telling them yet."

He paused again.

"And we're only telling you because we don't want you to think Mom is sick, and we need you to be helpful."

"Telling us what?" Andy shouted. "So far you haven't told us anything!"

"It's loose," Bruce said.

Andy coughed and kicked the side of his bed.

"What's that? Did you say something?" Mr. Russell asked.

Andy hit his chest and coughed again.

"No. I didn't say anything."

"Well," Mr. Russell went on, "don't tell this to anyone, not even any of your closest friends."

Andy's bed moved.

Andy looked down. A gerbil tail was sticking out from underneath the bed. Then the gerbil turned and it was looking up, right at Andy.

Andy glanced at his father, then at Rachel. Neither of them had noticed the gerbil. With hand signals, Andy told the gerbil to go under the bed. The gerbil tilted its head slightly. It didn't seem to understand.

"I know Mom doesn't look well now," Mr. Russell said. "That's because she has morning sickness. It's not serious. Women often get it during the first few months of pregnancy."

Mr. Russell looked at Andy and Rachel and smiled. "That's right. Mom is pregnant. We're going to have a baby."

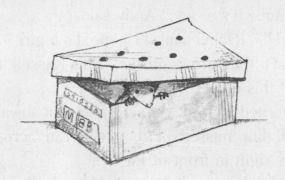

Chapter 5
Get It Away

A ndy looked away from the gerbil to his father. Mr. Russell was smiling broadly.

"Really?" Rachel asked.

Mr. Russell nodded.

"Oh, this is so exciting!" Rachel exclaimed.

"Mom better be careful," Andy warned. "With all that barfing, she might barf up the baby."

"Oh, Andy," Rachel said, "you can't barf a baby." Then she turned to her father and asked, "Do you know if it's a girl or a boy? Janet's mother had a baby and they knew it was going to be a girl. There's a test she took to find out."

"I hope it's a boy," Andy said.

"Well," Rachel said, "I hope it's a girl."

"Isn't this great news?" Mr. Russell asked. "Isn't this great?"

The bed moved. A hand shot out toward the gerbil but missed. The gerbil ran across the room, right in front of Rachel.

"Help! A mouse!" Rachel shouted. She quickly lifted her feet off the floor and then climbed onto Andy's desk, right on top of his pencils, markers, dinosaur collector cards, and used tissues.

The gerbil ran under the desk and into a corner of the room. Andy lay down on the floor and spread out his arms. The gerbil turned to one side and saw Andy's right hand waiting. It turned to the other side and saw Andy's left hand.

"Don't be afraid, little friend," Andy said. "I won't hurt you."

Andy moved closer, and as he did the gerbil looked straight at Andy and in a panic tried to run under him, but instead it ran right into Andy's shirt pocket. Andy got up, pulled the

gerbil out by its tail, held it in front of Rachel, and said, "This isn't a mouse. It's a gerbil."

Rachel waved her arms and shouted, "Get it away from me! Get it away!"

Bruce stuck his head out from under the bed and said, "Don't be afraid. Gerbils are really very friendly."

"Hey!" Rachel shouted. "Where did you come from?"

"I came from school," Bruce said as he slowly crawled out. "You saw me on the bus, remember? I'm helping Andy catch the gerbils."

"Ger*bils!*" Rachel said. "You mean there are more of them running around this house? Oh, you just wait. You just wait." She got off the desk. A tissue was stuck to the seat of her leggings. "Yuck," she said, and brushed it off. "Just wait until I tell Mom. She'll make you get rid of all of them and that snake, too, and then she'll really punish you."

Rachel took a step toward the door, but Mr. Russell stood in her way.

"You're not telling your mother anything about this. She already feels nauseous and this will only make her feel worse."

Rachel folded her arms and said, "Then you'll punish Andy and you'll get rid of his animals."

"No one is punishing Andy. His gerbils got loose and he's catching them. You can either help Andy and Bruce catch the gerbils or you can help me take care of your mother."

"That's what always happens around here. Andy gets away with everything," Rachel muttered. "I'll help you, Dad. I'll take care of Mom. I'd rather hold a barf basin than chase after mice."

"They're gerbils," Andy said.

"Whatever."

"And Bruce," Mr. Russell said, "what you heard in this room about a baby is a Russell family secret. Don't tell anyone."

"Don't worry," Bruce said, "I can keep a secret."

"Good," Mr. Russell said.

Andy was still holding on to the gerbil. "Here, hold him," Andy told Bruce. "I'll get something to put him in."

He turned and gave Bruce the gerbil.

"Hey," Rachel said. "Is that my autograph book in your back pocket?"

"Oh, yes," Andy said, and gave it to her. "I found it. Aren't you glad?"

Rachel opened the book and asked, "Did you tear these pages?"

Andy shook his head and mumbled, "The gerbils chewed on them."

"This is too much. This is just too much," Rachel said.

Then there was a faint call from Andy's parents' bedroom. "Charles, Charles, I need you."

"Rachel, come with me," Mr. Russell said as he turned to leave, "and don't you say a word about the gerbils."

"I'll try not to say anything," Rachel said, "but it won't be easy."

After Mr. Russell and Rachel left the room, Andy opened the closet door and took out an empty shoe box. He punched a few holes in the cover. Bruce put the gerbil in the box and Andy quickly put the top on.

Bruce said, "You're lucky your mother is pregnant. If she wasn't, Rachel would have told her about the gerbils and you would get in *real* trouble."

"I'm lucky," Andy said, "because I might get a brother."

Bruce smiled and said, "Adults get funny when they have a baby. I know my parents did when Danny was born. They made everyone be really quiet and they washed their hands a lot and every time Danny did something, they made a fuss like he was some kind of genius. They kept telling me to whisper, like Danny might listen to what I was saying."

"Bruce, they told you to whisper because they didn't want you to wake him."

"Oh."

Bruce kept talking about Danny, but Andy was no longer paying attention. He was thinking about having a baby in the house, having to whisper all the time, and that awful baby smell that Danny had.

He also thought about Tamika. Andy had hoped Tamika could live with them. But Bruce was right—adults *do* get funny when they have a baby. This was probably the very worst time to ask if Tamika could move in.

"And listen to this!" Bruce said.

Andy looked at his friend.

"I once changed Danny's yucky diaper and he squirted all over me. I had to change my shirt and everything."

"That's nice," Andy said.

"No, it's not," Bruce responded. "It's disgusting."

"Right, it's disgusting," Andy said, and held up the shoe box. "Let's put this gerbil in the tank with its friends and catch the others."

Chapter 6
The Trap

When they passed the door to Andy's parents' bedroom, Bruce smiled and said, "I hope you feel better, Mrs. Russell."

Andy looked in the room. Mr. Russell was standing by the window. He turned and looked at Bruce. Rachel was sitting on the floor, near the bed, holding the green basin. She looked up. Mrs. Russell looked, too, and gave Andy and Bruce a weak smile.

She doesn't look pregnant, Andy thought. *She*

just looks nauseous. Andy pulled on the back of Bruce's shirt and whispered, "Let's go."

"You may have the flu," Bruce continued. "My mother had it last year and for a few days she felt really bad."

Andy grabbed Bruce's arm and pulled him away from the door.

"What were you doing?" Andy asked when they were downstairs.

Bruce said, "I know about old people. They like it when you ask about their health."

Andy opened the basement door, pulled Bruce along, quickly closed the door behind them, and said, "You know my mother doesn't have the flu. She's pregnant."

"Now your mother thinks I don't know the Russell family secret. That's why I said that."

Andy just shook his head and walked down the basement steps. He opened the closet door, took out a flashlight, and turned it on. Then he crawled on the floor and pointed the light under the baseboard heater.

"I know the gerbils were here. They left droppings."

Andy crawled to the couch and looked under

there, too. Then he looked among the toys and books.

Ta. Ta. Ta.

"Did you hear that?" Andy whispered.

Bruce nodded.

"Where did it come from?"

Bruce pointed to the bookcase. "Behind there," I think.

Andy got on a chair and moved aside books and toys that were on top of the bookcase. Using the beam from the flashlight, he tried to look behind it, but he couldn't see anything. Andy got off the chair, returned it to its place by the table, went to the storage room, and came out with a ladder. He climbed the ladder and tried again to look behind the bookcase.

"I still can't see anything."

"I know," Bruce said, "but even if you saw one back there, how would you get it?"

Andy came down the ladder and sat on its bottom rung. He shook his head and said, "They're smaller than we are, but we should be smarter. There must be some way to catch the gerbils."

Bruce said, "Of course we're smarter than gerbils. We're in the fourth grade."

Bruce smiled. Then he said, "And don't worry. We'll catch all the gerbils."

"Thanks."

Andy sat on the bottom rung of the ladder for a while and thought. Then he went over to the two full gerbil tanks and looked in. Gerbils were playing on the exercise wheel and others were crawling through the long, twisted plastic tunnel to get to the food bowl.

"That's it!" Andy said, and clapped his hands. "We *won't* catch the gerbils. We'll outsmart them."

Andy returned the ladder to the storage room. Then he went upstairs. He looked into his parents' bedroom. Mr. Russell was patting Mrs. Russell's back while she leaned over the green basin. Rachel was holding the basin with one hand. She held her nose with her other hand, and her eyes were closed.

Andy went quickly to his room and emptied the wastebasket onto the floor. He kicked the trash under his bed, took the wastebasket to the basement, set it on the table, and filled it with gerbil food.

Andy put his face in the wastebasket and took a deep breath.

"Aah," Andy said. "The gerbils will smell that and say, 'Food! Let me get some.' This wastebasket is real deep. Once they get in, they won't be able to climb out."

Bruce asked, "But how will they get in?"

"Just watch."

Andy pulled back the screen from the top of one of the tanks. He took out the twisted plastic tunnel and then very carefully put the screen back on. He took the tunnels from the other tanks, too, and put them all on the floor.

"Can you help me take these apart?"

"Sure," Bruce said, "but why?"

"You'll see."

Andy and Bruce pulled and turned the plastic tubes until they had separated them all. Then they put the pieces together into one very long tunnel. Andy set one end over the wastebasket and the other on the floor. The tunnel was now one very long covered ramp leading to the food.

"What do we do now?" Bruce asked.

"We just wait," Andy told him. "The gerbils

will smell the food and run up the ramp to get it. They'll fall into the wastebasket and then be unable to get out. Then I'll put them in their tank, where they'll be safe and get plenty to eat."

Andy sat on the couch, folded his arms, watched the wastebasket, and waited. Bruce sat next to Andy, folded his arms, and watched and waited, too.

Chapter 7
She's My Friend

Andy stared at the wastebasket. Bruce looked at him, and waited to hear more about his gerbil-catching plan, but Andy was quiet.

"Do you think this will work?" Bruce asked.

"Of course," Andy answered without even turning to face his friend. "Why do you think I did it?"

Bruce was quiet for a minute. Then he asked, "How long do you think it will take?"

"I don't know," Andy answered, clearly impatient with Bruce's questions.

Bruce looked across the room at the ramp, the wastebasket, and the bookcase filled with books and toys. He knew he should be quiet, but he just couldn't be. "What are you thinking?" he asked.

"I'm thinking," Andy answered, again sounding annoyed, "when will you stop asking so many questions?" Then Andy said in a softer tone, "I'm also thinking about Ms. Roman, my mother, and Tamika."

Andy stared straight ahead as he talked. He spoke slowly and softly.

"This year has really been hard for Tamika. First her parents had that accident. Then the Perlmans took her in as a foster child until her parents get better. But now they have to go to South America and she can't go along."

"Why do they have to go there?" Bruce asked.

"They're anthropologists. They study people and they're doing some project for something they're writing."

"Why can't Tamika go?"

"You know she visits her parents every Sunday and she couldn't visit them if she went to South America. And the Perlmans will be moving around a lot. Tamika would have to keep changing schools."

"Oh."

Andy looked at Bruce and said, "You're my good friend."

"I'm your *best* friend," Bruce corrected him.

"Can you keep another secret?" Andy asked.

"I can keep lots of secrets," Bruce answered proudly.

"Well," Andy said, "the agency found a place for Tamika, and the new foster home is not in our district. So she'll have to leave our school. The secret is that I want her to live with us, so she can stay in our class with all her friends." Andy paused for a moment and then added, "Especially me."

"That would be nice," Bruce said. He thought about that for a while. Then he asked, "Would Tamika be your foster sister?"

Andy nodded.

Andy sat very still and stared at the gerbil tunnel for what seemed to Bruce to be a very long time. Tears formed in Andy's eyes as he spoke softly, almost to himself. "With the gerbils loose and Mom pregnant, this is a bad time to ask my parents if Tamika can live here."

Tears rolled down Andy's cheeks. Bruce sat next to him and waited.

"And if Ms. Roman sees Mom at that meeting next week and says something bad about me, my parents will never let Tamika stay, and that's not fair." Andy wiped his cheeks with the back of his hand. "It's not Tamika's fault I wasn't paying attention in class, or the gerbils got loose, or my mom is pregnant."

Bruce turned his wrist slowly and glanced down at his watch. It was four o'clock. He would have to go home in half an hour and they still hadn't done their homework.

"I have to find out soon if Tamika can stay here, before the people at the agency send her to live with that other family." Andy slowly stood, pulled the shirttail out of his pants, wiped his eyes with it, and said, "I'm going to ask Dad now, before something else happens."

"Should I go with you?" Bruce asked.

"No. You stay here and watch for gerbils. I have to do this alone."

Andy went up the basement stairs. He quickly opened then closed the door behind him so no gerbils could get upstairs. He walked past the kitchen and saw that Rachel was back at the table, doing her homework.

"Is Mom better?" Andy asked.

Rachel looked up. "She's a little better. She said I should do my homework." She paused for a moment. Then she said, "Don't worry. I won't tell Mom about the gerbils, and I looked at my autograph book and they didn't chew so much. But you'd better not let them chew up anything else of mine."

"I won't," Andy promised.

Andy went upstairs to look for his father. He looked first in his parents' room. His mother was in bed, with her clothes and shoes still on. Her right arm was folded over her eyes and the barf basin was on the floor next to the bed.

Andy thought, *Dad has a real hard time saying no to me. First I'll get him to say Tamika can stay with us. Then I'll ask Mom and Rachel. Or better yet, he'll ask them.*

Andy looked in his bedroom and Rachel's room for his father, but he didn't find him. Andy went back to the door of his parents' bedroom.

"Hey, Mom, do you know where Dad is?"

Mrs. Russell slowly lifted her left hand and pointed to her closet.

"He's in the closet?"

Mrs. Russell nodded.

Andy opened the door to his mother's closet and looked in. There were racks of his mother's dresses and slacks on either side of the door, with shelves filled with neatly labeled boxes above each of the racks. In the middle of the closet was a rope ladder hanging down from the ceiling. Andy looked up and saw that the hatchway to the attic was open.

Andy climbed the bottom two rungs of the ladder and called, "Are you up there, Dad?"

"Yes."

"I need to talk to you, Dad."

"Come on up."

Andy hated climbing the shaky rope ladder

and going in the cramped, musty attic, but he had to if he was going to ask his father about Tamika. Andy looked up at the open hatchway, held on to the ladder, carefully lifted his right foot onto the first rung and then his left onto the next. He climbed the next three rungs, reached up, held on to the sides of the hatchway, and pulled himself up into the attic.

"Hey, Andy."

Andy leaned over the opening and looked at the ladder as it turned and swung freely. He dreaded having to reach with his foot later to try and find the top rung and make his way back down into his mother's closet. Going down was worse than going up.

Andy turned to his dad, who was crouched in the corner where the sloping roof and bare wood floor met.

"Hey, Dad."

Mr. Russell was holding a pad of paper in a clipboard and one end of a metal tape measure. He pushed the automatic rewind switch and twelve feet of tape raced across the attic floor and into the case. Mr. Russell wrote down some numbers and then told Andy, "I'm thinking of adding

a room up here. With the baby and all, we could use an extra bedroom."

"I need to talk to you, Dad."

"In a minute."

Andy sat on the attic floor and watched his father measure the height of the roof in different parts of the attic. Mr. Russell made chalk marks on the floor and measured the distance from one chalk mark to the next. He wrote some notes. Then he hooked the tape measure to his belt.

Mr. Russell smiled.

"Here's my plan: The stairs will start in the hall and go through Mom's closet. For the windows, I'll break through the roof and build dormers. I'll do it after work and you can help."

"Can we build two bedrooms up here?"

"We don't need two more rooms. We only need one."

"That's why I want to talk to you, Dad." Andy paused. He didn't know what to say.

Mr. Russell walked over and sat on the floor next to Andy. "Is it about the baby?"

Andy shook his head and said, "It's not about the baby."

"The gerbils?"

Andy shook his head. "It's really about Tamika, but first I have to tell you about Ms. Roman."

"This sounds complicated," Mr. Russell said, and smiled.

"Ms. Roman called on me today and I didn't know the answer."

"That's not so terrible, Andy. You can't be expected to know the answer to every question."

"But, Dad, I didn't even know we were doing math. I thought we were doing geography. The answer was some number and I said, 'China.'"

"Oh."

"Dad, I try to listen in class, but she's so boring and she hates me. She only calls on me when I'm thinking about something else."

Andy looked at the floor and said, "I was thinking about Tamika, Dad. Her parents are still in the hospital and the Perlmans have to go to South America."

"Is she going with them?"

"She can't," Andy said slowly. "They'll be moving around a lot and Tamika needs to stay in one place so she can go to school." Andy paused. Then he said softly, "The foster agency found a place for her, but if she lives there she'll have to change schools. If she lives here, she won't have to move anywhere, just next door, and she will stay with me in Ms. Roman's class."

"Here?" Mr. Russell asked. "In this house?"

"She could sleep in Rachel's room, in the extra bed, or when the new room is ready, she could sleep up here."

"We're having a baby. We have no room for someone else."

There were tears in Andy's eyes and they were spilling onto his cheeks. "She's not someone else," Andy said, trying to keep himself from crying. "She's my friend."

Mr. Russell took Andy's hand. He didn't speak for what seemed to Andy to be a long while. Then he said, "Tamika is a nice girl."

Andy nodded.

"And that accident was a real tragedy."

Andy hoped his father was about to say Tamika could live with them. He didn't.

Mr. Russell said, "But what makes you think Rachel would want to share her room? And you see how your mother feels. This is really not a good time for us to have a guest."

"Rachel and Tamika are friends," Andy told his

father. "And Mom's not really sick. She's just pregnant."

Mr. Russell gently held Andy's hand. "I'll speak to your mother," he said, "and I'll speak to Rachel."

"Sure, Dad," Andy said, not hiding his disappointment. He wiped the tears from his cheeks. "You'll ask Mom and Rachel. That's just another way of saying no."

"That's not true at all," Mr. Russell said. "It's a way of saying I can't decide something like this on my own. It wouldn't be fair to the other people who live in this house. I'll speak with your mother, but not until she feels better, and I'll speak to Rachel."

Mr. Russell let go of Andy's hand. They just sat there, quietly, for a while. Then Mr. Russell got up and stood over the hatchway. Before he stepped down he asked, "What about the gerbils? Did you get them all?"

"Yikes!" Andy exclaimed. "I left Bruce in the basement!"

Chapter 8
Lots of Ways to Say No

Mr. Russell started down the ladder.

"And we didn't even begin our homework," Andy said. "But, I promise, I'll do it all and I'll listen in class, and if Ms. Roman sees Mom at that meeting next week, she'll say how good I am and that I get every answer right."

Mr. Russell reached for Andy. With his father to help him, it was easy going down the rope ladder.

As they stepped out of the closet, Mr. Russell

put his finger to his lips. Mrs. Russell was sleeping.

Andy was careful not to wake her. Before he left the room, he stopped for a moment and looked at his mother. He wondered what she had inside—his brother or his sister?

Then Andy hurried to the basement. He found Bruce there, still sitting on the couch. Bruce's eyes opened wide as soon as Andy closed the door. He stretched out his arms and called across the basement in a loud, excited whisper.

"You should have been here. It was great! A gerbil came out from the toys. It smelled the food. Its nose was twitching like this."

Bruce wrinkled his nose in an effort to show Andy how the gerbil's nose twitched. But he seemed more like someone who was about to sneeze.

"It looked in the wastebasket, then at the tunnel, and then it looked at me. I sat here real still. I didn't want to scare the gerbil. I pretended I was a large stuffed animal."

Bruce held his hands up, signaling the coming triumphant end to his story. "It crawled through the tunnel and fell into the food. I left the gerbil there so you would know I'm not making any of this up."

Andy looked in the wastebasket. A gerbil was in there, happily eating. Andy grabbed its tail and put the gerbil in the middle tank.

"Isn't that great?" Bruce asked.

"Yeah, it's great," Andy answered. "But, we're still missing two, so we'll leave the trap."

Bruce looked at his watch. It was past five.

"I have to go home now. I'm already late for dinner."

"Please," Andy said, "don't go yet. We haven't even started our homework. Call your parents and ask if you can stay here longer. Ask if you can stay for dinner."

Bruce made the call. He spoke to his mother. Then he listened for a while and said, "Sure, Mom," and hung up the telephone.

"My mother said I should remember to thank your parents for dinner," Bruce told Andy, "and that I should be polite."

Andy said, "You're always polite."

"Thank you."

"See that! You even thanked me for saying you're polite."

Andy and Bruce spread their schoolbooks on the floor. Then Andy told Bruce, "My dad said he has to ask Mom and Rachel if Tamika can stay here. That's like saying 'No way!'"

Andy shook his head and said sadly, "Adults have lots of ways to say no."

"Yeah," Bruce said. "My mom's favorite way is 'I'll think about it.' That means no. And 'Maybe later.' That means no, too."

Then Bruce told Andy, "Tamika is real nice. She's good at making friends. She'll be OK."

"I hope you're right," Andy said.

They sat quietly for a while. Then Andy said, "Let's do math first. We'll work separately and compare our answers. If we get the same answers, they're probably right."

Andy and Bruce did the math that way, and the science, too. They were closing their books when Mr. Russell opened the basement door.

"Oh, hi, Bruce. I didn't know you were still here." He looked at the plastic tunnel and the wastebasket and asked, "What's all this?"

Bruce explained about the trap and told Mr. Russell how it had caught a gerbil. He even tried again to twitch his nose like one.

"Oh my," Mr. Russell teased. "When you do that, you look like a gerbil."

"I was just showing you what the gerbil did when it smelled the food."

"Oh," Mr. Russell said. Then he told Andy, "Mom feels better, so we're going to eat now. I made pizza muffins for us and toast for Mom."

Andy told his father, "Bruce's mother already said he can eat with us. Can he, Dad?"

"Sure!" Mr. Russell said. "Put your books away and come upstairs."

Andy and Bruce put their books in their backpacks. Then, as they were going up the basement stairs, Andy told Bruce, "Mom feels good enough to eat toast, so she must be better. At dinner maybe Dad will ask her about Tamika."

Chapter 9
"What?"

Mrs. Russell was sitting by the kitchen table with her legs stretched out, her arms hanging by her sides, and her head resting on the back of the chair. Rachel was sitting next to her, gently patting her mother's hand.

As they came into the kitchen, Bruce whispered to Andy, "Your mother doesn't look so good."

The boys sat down, and Mr. Russell gave each

of them two pizza muffins. The boys ate quietly and watched Mrs. Russell.

She leaned forward and took the piece of toast off her plate. She looked at it. She turned it over and looked at it some more. Then she nibbled on it and sighed.

Mr. Russell leaned forward and asked, "How is it?"

"It's very good."

"Would you like some hot tea?"

Mrs. Russell slowly nodded, "Yes, please," she said. "Herbal tea."

Mr. Russell turned on the burner under the teakettle and took a mug from the shelf above the sink. As he reached for it, he looked up. He paused. Then he turned to Andy and pointed to the ceiling. Mr. Russell had seen the handprint.

Oh, please, Andy thought, *don't say anything. I don't want Mom to know about it.*

Mrs. Russell was resting her head on the back of her chair again. Rachel was cutting her pizza muffin into bite-size pieces. Neither of them saw Mr. Russell point to himself, then open his hand,

and move it in a circle. Bruce was watching, but Andy didn't care. Bruce was his friend.

Andy shook his head. He didn't know what his father was telling him.

Mr. Russell did it all again. He pointed to himself and moved his open hand in another circle.

Andy still didn't understand.

"He said he'll clean it later," Bruce whispered.

Andy looked at his father. Mr. Russell nodded.

"Clean what?" Rachel asked.

"Nothing," Mr. Russell told her. "I'm just about to make the tea."

He poured boiling water from the kettle into the mug. Then he dipped a tea bag into the water.

Rachel watched her father make the tea. Then she leaned forward and asked her mother, "Would you like some jelly on your toast?"

"Yes, please."

Rachel went to the refrigerator for the jelly.

"Can Tamika live here?" Andy asked quickly.

Mr. Russell dropped the tea bag into the water and frowned at Andy. Rachel turned from the refrigerator.

"What?" Mrs. Russell asked.

"It would only be for a year, until the Perlmans get back from South America. It may even be less, if Tamika's parents get better."

"What?" Mrs. Russell asked again.

"Hey, that wouldn't be fair," Rachel said. "Why can Andy have a friend living here and I can't?"

Andy glared at Rachel "Because *my* friend needs a place to live!" he told her.

"*Your* friend!" Rachel shouted. "Tamika is *my* friend!"

Rachel put the jar of strawberry jelly on the table. Then she said again slowly, "Hey, Tamika *is* my friend, too."

Mrs. Russell put her hands to her ears and said, "Quiet, please!"

Mrs. Russell tapped on her plate with her fork to get her husband's attention and asked, "What's this all about?"

Mr. Russell set the mug of tea on the table, sat next to Mrs. Russell, and explained, "Tamika needs a new place to live. Her parents are still in the hospital and the Perlmans are going away."

"Rachel wants her here," Andy said quickly. "And I want her. And Dad already said she can stay here, so you're the only one left who has to say yes."

"Wait a minute! Wait a minute!" Mr. Russell said. "I never said Tamika can stay here. I said I had to discuss this with your mother."

"Where would she sleep?" Mrs. Russell asked.

Andy said, "She could sleep in the basement."

"With the mice?" Rachel asked.

"They're gerbils," Andy told her.

"Whatever," Rachel said. Then she added, "She can sleep in my room. I have an extra bed."

Mrs. Russell shook her head and said slowly, "But we can't take in someone else now because …" She looked at Bruce. "Because …," she said again, and stopped.

Mr. Russell told her, "Bruce knows about the baby."

"He does?"

"Bruce was under Andy's bed when Dad told us you're pregnant," Rachel explained.

Andy looked at his mother. He didn't want her to ask why Bruce was under his bed, so he quickly said, "This all happened when you were barfing. But you look much better now. How do you feel?"

She smiled. "I feel better, thank you. But I do wish you'd be more careful with the words you use. *Barfing* is not a nice word."

Mrs. Russell took a sip of tea and then asked Andy, "Does Tamika know you planned to ask us if she can stay here?"

"Yes, and she really wants to because if she lives with the family the agency found for her, she'll have to change schools. And she might not like her new foster parents, and there are children in that family, and she might not like them, either."

Mrs. Russell shook her head again and said, "You should have asked Dad and me *before* you spoke to Tamika."

Mrs. Russell took another sip of tea. She reached out across the table and patted Andy's hand. She smiled and said, "Of course, we have to tell her she can't live here, but we have to do it gently. Why don't we have her come for dinner tomorrow, so we can explain."

"She's so nice," Andy said. There were tears

in his eyes again. "She's my friend," he said, and wiped his eyes. "And she needs us."

"She really is nice," Rachel said.

"I wish we could help her," Mr. Russell said. "Maybe we can help her find some other place to stay."

"I'll ask my friends," Rachel said. "We all like Tamika."

They sat quietly for a while. Finally, Mr. Russell turned to Bruce and said, "Why don't you finish eating and then I'll take you home."

Chapter 10
Pay Attention

Andy stayed up much of the night, wondering what he would tell Tamika. He just *had* to tell her his mother was pregnant. He'd tell her that his mother was sick, barfing all over the place. Maybe then Tamika would understand why she couldn't stay with them.

Then Andy remembered it was a Russell family secret that his mother was going to have a baby. Actually, now it was a Russell-family-and-Bruce secret. Andy didn't know what to do.

The next morning Andy went into the basement to check the wastebasket trap. He found one gerbil in there and put it in the middle tank.

Andy looked at all the gerbils and thought about how crowded they were in the three tanks. The first two gerbils had been fun, but with so many, he was sure they would get him in trouble again. Andy knew he had to find new homes for them. But where? Andy checked the tops of each tank, to be sure the screens were on right. Then he went outside to wait for the bus.

Tamika was late again. She ran up the stairs and into the bus just as Mr. Cole was about to close the door. When she got to the back and sat next to Andy, he knew he should tell her that his parents said she couldn't live with them. But his mother had said *she* would explain. So Andy just told Tamika, "I spoke to my parents last night and they want you to come to dinner."

"Really? That's great! If they want me to come to dinner that means they might want to become my foster parents. Oh, that's so great!"

Andy looked at Tamika. Her happy smile brightened her whole face. Andy didn't know how he could tell her that his parents had invited her to say they *couldn't* be her foster parents.

"Did they say where I'd sleep?" Tamika asked. "I guess I'll be in Rachel's room. Does she mind?"

Andy shook his head. He looked down at the floor of the bus and thought, *Let Mom and Dad tell Tamika why she can't live with us!*

"Did they say when I could move in?" Tamika asked.

"Let's not talk about that now," Andy said, "because...well, just because."

"Sure," Tamika said. "We can talk about it at dinner."

"Sure," Andy mumbled. He was glad Bruce was sitting far enough away not to hear the conversation.

When the bus got to school, Andy, Tamika, and Bruce hurried to their classroom. Ms. Roman was standing by the door. She smiled at Andy and said, "Do you remember what you promised? You said today you would pay attention in class."

"Yes, I did," Andy told her, "and I will. I really will."

Andy sat in his seat and wondered how he could possibly listen to Ms. Roman all day. He was sure she was the worst teacher ever. She was surely the most boring teacher he had ever had. He watched her go to the chair by her desk and sit down. Andy knew what was coming. She would check the attendance and then start talking. She would talk on and on.

How can I stay awake? Andy asked himself.

He bent down and retied his sneakers. He tied them really tight, so his feet were uncomfortable. He tightened his belt, too. *Good,* he thought, *maybe my aching feet and stomach will keep me focused on Ms. Boring Roman.* Next, Andy wrote on the cover of his notebook PAY ATTENTION! and WAKE UP! in large block letters.

All during class he tried to listen to Ms. Roman explain about multiplication, but he kept thinking about Tamika instead. In the middle of the math lesson, Ms. Roman looked at Andy. She smiled, so Andy did, too.

"Well, Andrew, what's the answer?"

Andy looked at the chalkboard. It was covered with numbers. He looked down at his notebook, pretending to be checking his work. "Five hundred and fourteen?" Andy said.

"I know! I know!" Stacy Ann Jackson called out.

"Yes, Stacy Ann," Ms. Roman said.

"Sixteen thousand, nine hundred."

"That's right."

Well, Andy thought, *at least I answered with a number and not the name of a country.*

As soon as Ms. Roman turned to write something on the chalkboard, Stacy Ann smiled and whispered to Andy, "*I* pay attention in class and *I* do my work."

Andy thought of lots of things to answer Stacy Ann, but he didn't want to get into more trouble with Ms. Roman, so he just stuck out his tongue.

Andy was relieved when Ms. Roman announced it was time for lunch. It was difficult to pretend for so long to be a good, attentive student.

Before he left the classroom, Andy loosened his belt and his sneaker laces. In the cafeteria he sat with Tamika and Bruce. Bruce opened his lunch bag and took out a sandwich, two containers of orange juice, a bag of cookies, and an

apple. He shook his head and sighed, "My mom never gives me enough."

"Here," Andy told him. He took a small bag of pretzels from his lunch bag and gave the rest to Bruce. "Have a party."

As Tamika unwrapped her sandwich, she told Andy, "I think I'll wear my fancy dress tonight."

Andy pushed a straw into the chocolate milk container, and as he took a sip he said, "That's nice."

Bruce was busy eating. Andy was glad he didn't tell Tamika that she couldn't live with the Russells. *He really is good at keeping secrets,* Andy thought.

When they returned to class, Ms. Roman told Andy, "You were really very good this morning. I was pleased."

Andy wanted Ms. Roman to still be pleased at the end of the day. When he got to his seat, he sat down and took off his left sneaker. He broke the eraser off his pencil and dropped it in his sneaker. Then he put the shoe on and tied it. He put his left foot down. *Good,* Andy thought. *It hurts. Now, any time I start to daydream, I'll stomp my foot. That should wake me.*

Andy stomped his left foot twice during the geography lesson and three more times during science. Just before dismissal, Ms. Roman talked about the school carnival. Andy didn't have to stomp his foot then. He thought working on a carnival for charity was exciting. Ms. Roman still wanted suggestions for fun booths, as well as donations of old books and toys for prizes.

Bruce raised his hand and said, "I have some toy cars I don't use anymore. I can give you those."

"That would be nice," Ms. Roman said.

Andy thought that winning Bruce's old broken toy cars would be more like losing. Some of them had no wheels. He remembered the carnival he had gone to at the firehouse. He had tried to toss Ping-Pong balls into little goldfish bowls. If he'd got one in, he would have won a goldfish. Now, that's a prize!

"And I can bring in some books I no longer read," Stacy Ann Jackson said.

Suddenly Andy had a great idea.

"We can give away gerbils," Andy called out. "They're great pets. A gerbil is an even better prize than a goldfish because they go through mazes and have babies. What do you think, Ms. Roman? I can bring in lots of them."

Ms. Roman smiled. "That's a good idea," she said.

Andy was standing now. "Whoever wins one will just have to promise to take care of his gerbil and to love it. That's all I ask," he said.

Ms. Roman was excited by Andy's idea. "If your parents agree to give up some of your gerbils, I think we have our prizes."

"Oh, my parents will say yes," Andy said. "I'm sure of that."

When they got on the bus, Bruce asked Andy if he would give him a gerbil. "I'm not sure I'll be able to win one."

"Sure," Andy told Bruce. "If I give away the rest of them as prizes, I can even let you have one of the tanks."

Tamika told Andy, "Giving the gerbils as prizes is a great idea." She smiled. "It's brilliant, Andy. Simply brilliant."

Bruce wasn't coming to Andy's house, so he got off at his regular stop. Andy, Tamika, Rachel, and the Belmonts got off at the next stop.

Tamika told Andy, "I decided I *will* wear my

flower dress for dinner. It's my best one. My mom bought it for me just before the accident."

After they crossed the street, she said to Andy, "I'll see you at about five." Then she told Rachel, "And I'll see you, too."

"I don't know why she's so happy," Rachel said. "Doesn't she know Dad is making dinner, so it'll be pizza muffins again or his yucky meat loaf. The last time the meat was raw and I found a shirt button in my piece."

Andy told his sister, "She thinks Mom and Dad will tell her she can move in with us."

"Oh," Rachel said.

Andy watched Tamika go into the house next door. He didn't care what was for dinner. He just hoped Tamika's new foster family would be as nice to her as the Perlmans had been.

Chapter 11
We Have to Talk

R achel unlocked the front door and went
straight to the kitchen. She opened her
backpack, took out her schoolbooks, and put
them on the table. Then she sat down to do her
homework.

Andy dropped his backpack on the floor by the
front door and went downstairs to check his gerbil trap. He found one gerbil in there. He put it
in the middle tank.

That should be all of them, he thought. Andy

counted seven gerbils, but he wasn't sure if there were six and he had counted one twice, or if there were really seven. He counted again. Seven. He had them all.

Andy took the long tunnel apart and put pieces back into each of the tanks. He knew he should reassemble them into the twisted tunnels the gerbils loved, but he didn't have time. He had to prepare for Tamika's visit.

Andy went to the kitchen.

"You have to go somewhere else. I have to set the table," he told Rachel. "Tamika is coming."

"Andy," Rachel said. "You're making too much of this dinner. Mom and Dad already decided Tamika can't live here. And anyway, I do my homework in the kitchen. If you want to set the table, do it in the dining room."

Andy decided not to argue with Rachel. Tamika was "company," so they would eat in the dining room. He would set the table real fancy, like the time Mom's boss, Mr. Kamen, the principal of the high school, came.

Andy opened the cupboard and took out five place mats, five fancy dinner plates, and five salad plates. He got flatware from the drawer, napkins, and the salt and pepper shakers. He set everything on the dining-room table, then cut out five paper squares, folded them, and made place cards. Andy wrote MOM, DAD, ANDY, RACHEL, and TAMIKA on the cards, one name to a card. Beside each name, even Rachel's, he drew a large red heart. He set each card on a plate. He put Tamika's plate next to his.

Andy checked to be sure everything was right. Dinner plates, salad plates, napkins, knives, forks, spoons. He looked at the table for a while and it seemed to him something was missing, but he didn't know what.

Andy sat in his seat and imagined he was eating spaghetti. He pretended to sprinkle on some pepper. Then he reached for his fork, dug into the mound of imaginary spaghetti, and twirled it around. One strand was dangling. It just wouldn't stay with the others, so Andy took the knife and cut it. Then Andy opened his mouth wide and pretended to eat.

Andy chewed for a while. Then he looked across the table to one of the empty chairs and asked, "What are you pointing at, Mom?" He looked down at his shirt and said, "Yikes! Tomato sauce!" He reached for his napkin and wiped it across his shirt.

Andy imagined he'd finished eating the entire mound of spaghetti. He put the fork and knife down, and just as he started to reach across his dinner plate for something to drink, he realized what was missing. Glasses.

Andy got up, went to the kitchen, and took the fancy glasses from the cabinet, the ones with the large $\mathcal{R}$ etched in the middle. He was putting them out when the front door opened. Andy's parents were home. Mrs. Russell looked tired as she walked toward the stairs.

"Hi, Mom!" called Rachel as her mother passed the kitchen.

"Hello," she answered in a faint voice.

Mrs. Russell looked in the dining room. She watched Andy put out the glasses. Then she asked, "What are you doing? Why did you take out our best glasses and dishes? And why aren't we eating in the kitchen?"

"Did you forget, Mom? Tamika is coming for dinner."

"Oh yes, how could I forget?" Mrs. Russell asked. "I wish I could prepare the meal, but I'm too tired to cook and I'm still a little nauseous. Your father will make dinner. I hope you told Tamika not to expect anything special."

Rachel was standing by the kitchen door. "Why should Andy say that?" she asked. "We'll prepare a feast."

"Just don't make a mess," Mrs. Russell said, and then started upstairs.

"Wait! Wait, Mom," Andy said suddenly. "I just remembered. I have some great news, great for you, at least. I may be giving my gerbils away as prizes at my school's charity carnival."

Mrs. Russell stopped and looked at Andy. Then she smiled and said, "That *is* great news. Whenever I think of all those gerbils living in the basement, I have this terrible fear that one day they might get out and be all over the house."

"Do you, Mom?" Rachel asked. "I get night-mares about that. I imagine gerbils everywhere, even under our beds, with Andy and his friends crawling after them. *Ooh!*" Rachel shook her shoulders as if she was horrified.

Andy glared at Rachel. Then he told his mother, "If I give them away at the carnival, we won't have to worry about that."

Mrs. Russell smiled and went slowly upstairs.

Mr. Russell handed Andy a box from the bakery and said, "Here's the dessert. Please put this in the kitchen." Then he looked in the dining room and said, "Well, I see the table is set. Who wants to help me cook? I'm making my surprise meat loaf."

Andy said, "I'll help, Dad. I'll make sure you cook the meat long enough."

"And I'll make the salad," Rachel said.

Andy, Rachel, and Mr. Russell went into the kitchen.

"What's the surprise?" Andy asked.

"You'll see."

Mr. Russell opened a cookbook to the meat-loaf page and put it on the counter near Andy, along with a metal loaf pan and a mixing bowl, a package of chopped beef, a raw egg, an onion, a box of bread crumbs, a can of tomato sauce, salt and pepper, a knife, and a measuring cup.

Andy emptied the package of chopped meat into the bowl. He squeezed the meat and smiled as it oozed through his fingers. It reminded him of making mud pies when he had been much younger. It had been fun making the pies, even though nobody would eat them. Andy rolled the meat into three balls and made a snowman, a *meat*man!

"What are you doing?" his father asked.

Andy answered, "I'm mixing the meat."

"What are you mixing it with?"

"My hands." Andy held up his two meat-covered hands.

"Yuck!" Rachel said. She was cutting a tomato into perfect wedges and carefully putting them into a wooden bowl.

"I meant," Mr. Russell said slowly, "are you mixing the meat with the egg and onion and other ingredients or are you just playing?"

Rachel answered, "He's just playing."

"I asked Andy," Mr. Russell said.

"I was just playing," Andy said. He shook the beef off his hands and into the bowl. Then he washed his hands in the sink.

Mr. Russell beat the egg, chopped the onion, and added them to the meat. He poured in bread crumbs and the can of tomato sauce, then tossed in a pinch of salt and pepper. Andy mixed it all together with his hands.

While Andy dumped the mixture into the loaf

pan and pressed it into shape, Mr. Russell worked on his surprise—two hard-boiled eggs that he set deep in the center of the meat loaf. "It'll look nice when I cut a slice and inside is a circle of yellow yolk surrounded by a circle of egg white."

Andy said, "I think one of the stacking clowns in the middle would be a better surprise, or I could write lots of little fortunes and stick them in there. Instead of fortune cookies, we would have fortune meat loaf. I'll write things like 'A tall handsome stranger will do your homework' and 'You will sit on a frog and be hoppy' and 'You will find a new home with friends.'"

Mr. Russell said, "Eggs are a good surprise," and he put the meat loaf in the oven.

He and Andy were preparing corn and potatoes when Tamika arrived. She was wearing her pretty flower-print dress and had a red ribbon in her hair. She gave Mr. Russell a bouquet of flowers and a large, covered plastic bowl, and said, "Thank you for inviting me."

Rachel was standing in the doorway to the kitchen. She was holding the wooden bowl with the salad she had made.

"These flowers are beautiful," Mr. Russell said.

"Mrs. Perlman told me to pick them for you," Tamika said. "They're from her yard."

"What's in the bowl?" Andy asked.

"I made salad for everyone."

Rachel held up the wooden bowl and said, "So did I."

Mr. Russell looked at Rachel, then at Tamika. "Why don't you mix them together," he suggested.

The two girls looked at each other for a moment. Then they smiled. Tamika poured her salad into the wooden bowl. Rachel tossed the two salads together.

Andy looked in the bowl and told Tamika, "I can tell which tomatoes Rachel cut and which are yours. Rachel's are all the same. Yours are all different sizes."

"I like diversity," Tamika said.

"What?" Andy asked.

Tamika explained, "I like it when things are not all the same."

Mr. Russell put the flowers in a vase and set it in the middle of the dining-room table.

RRRR!

The timer rang. Mr. Russell said, "Excuse me," went into the kitchen, and turned off the oven. He put on large cloth mitts, took out the meat loaf, and told Andy, Rachel, and Tamika, "Why don't you go to the bathroom and wash your hands and then sit down while I get Mom."

Andy said to Tamika, "I helped make the meat loaf." He showed her a trace of raw beef caught beneath his fingernails. "Chopped-up, mushed-up cow," he told her just before he washed it out.

"It's fun squeezing chopped meat with your hands, isn't it?" Tamika asked.

"Yeah," Andy said as he washed his hands. He shook off the water, went into the dining room, and sat down. Rachel and Tamika washed and dried their hands. They, too, entered the dining room. Rachel sat, but Tamika stood behind her chair.

"Why don't you sit?" Rachel asked.

"I'm waiting for the host and hostess."

"Are you talking about my parents?" Andy asked.

Tamika nodded.

Andy and Rachel got up and waited, too, with their hands on the back of their chairs. When

Mr. and Mrs. Russell entered the dining room, Mrs. Russell looked at Andy, Rachel, and Tamika for a moment. Then she smiled and said, "Hello, Tamika. How are you?"

"I'm just fine, Mrs. Russell."

"Are you standing to be polite?" Mrs. Russell asked.

"Yes," Tamika answered.

"How nice." Mrs. Russell pulled out her chair and sat down.

"I'm not standing to be polite," Andy explained as he and Rachel pulled out their chairs and sat down, too. "I was standing because she was."

Mrs. Russell noticed the flowers. "Oh, Charles, that was so sweet. I love flowers."

Andy said, "Tamika brought them and some of the salad, too. She mixed her salad with the one Rachel made."

"Oh my, that wasn't at all necessary, but very much appreciated." Mrs. Russell smiled. "I wish my children would learn to be such polite and thoughtful guests."

"See, Mom," Andy said. "Tamika can teach us lots of good stuff."

"Do you really think so?" Tamika asked.

Mr. Russell clapped his hands and said, "Let's eat!"

Rachel and Tamika served the salad on the small plates. Mrs. Russell said it was delicious.

"At my house," Tamika said, "we used to take turns making supper. Mom and Dad made real food, but I kept making the same thing—peanut butter sandwiches. Mom was tired of eating sandwiches, so she taught me to make salads. When I put some tuna in the salad, it's a whole meal."

"I love tuna in a salad," Mrs. Russell said. "It's delicious, and taking turns preparing meals is a great idea. Maybe we should do that."

"And whoever made the meal at my house cleaned the pots and dishes. That's one reason I make sandwiches and salads. There's very little mess."

"Well," Mr. Russell said as he got up, "who's ready for my surprise meat loaf?"

"I know the surprise," Andy said.

Mr. Russell brought in a bowl of corn and a large platter with the meat loaf surrounded by baby potatoes. He cut a slice of meat loaf and held it up for everyone to see. "Surprise!" he called out when they all saw the egg in the middle.

"That's so pretty," Tamika said.

Mr. Russell gave Rachel, Andy, and Tamika a slice. Rachel leaned really close and looked at the meat on her plate. "And so cooked," she said.

Mrs. Russell only ate potatoes. When she finished them, she asked Tamika, "How are your parents?"

"They're getting better, but very slowly. I don't know when they'll get to go home."

Mr. Russell leaned forward and said, "We know you'd like to stay here for a while, but . . ."

Mrs. Russell interrupted her husband. "But we still have to talk about it."

Andy looked at his mother. He wondered what there was to talk about. She had already decided she and his dad couldn't be Tamika's foster parents.

"Well, if we have to talk about it, we'll talk," Mr. Russell said. "Meanwhile, I'll clear the table and we can have the apple pie I brought home for dessert."

Tamika took her plate and Andy's, got up, and said, "I'll help."

"No," Mr. Russell said, and took the plates from her. "You just sit. You're our guest. Andy and Rachel will help."

Chapter 12
The Andersons

After dessert everyone helped clean up. Then Tamika thanked the Russells again for inviting her. "And thank you for the delicious meal," she said. As Andy walked with her to the door, she whispered to him, "Your mother said she has to think about letting me live here. I think that means yes."

"It could also mean no," Andy whispered. "When parents say they have to think about something, that's what it usually means."

"I hope you're wrong," Tamika said. Then she said, "Good-bye," and left.

Andy returned to the kitchen to talk to his parents, but only Rachel was there. She was eating the leftover apple pie.

"Where are Mom and Dad?" Andy asked.

Rachel's mouth was filled with pie. She pointed with her fork to the ceiling. Andy looked up and saw his handprint there. He hoped his father would get it off before his mother noticed it.

"Where are they?" Andy asked again.

"In their room," Rachel said with her mouth still full of pie.

Andy hurried up the stairs. The door to his parents' bedroom was closed, but he could hear them talking. He tiptoed to the door and listened.

"She's such a nice girl," his mother said. "And I don't think she'll be any trouble. Both Rachel and Andy like her. I expect Rachel and Andy to help with the baby. Maybe Tamika would help, too."

"I'm sure she would," Mr. Russell said.

"And Tamika is so polite. Andy is right. Maybe she'll teach him and Rachel 'good stuff.' "

Andy put his ear against the door.

"And," Mrs. Russell continued, "I know I said this before, but she really is such a nice girl. I think I'd like having her live here."

Andy's parents were quiet for a while. *Maybe they're reading,* Andy thought, *or getting undressed.* Andy waited by the door. Then he heard his father say, "I don't think we can simply decide to take her in. We have to be sure she still wants to stay here. And the foster agency probably has to approve us."

"Maybe we can take turns making dinner," Mrs. Russell said. "That's what Tamika and her parents used to do. With her, there would be five of us, so each of us would prepare dinner just once every five days." Then she said, "I do think Tamika would be a good influence on Rachel and Andy."

Mr. Russell asked, "Are you sure you want this extra responsibility, especially now?"

"Yes, I'm sure."

"Then we have to talk with Rachel and Andy. First we have to be sure Rachel is willing to share her room. And we have to ask Andy if he still wants Tamika to live here."

Andy heard his father get up from the bed. He

ran to his room. He had just reached it when he heard his parents' bedroom door open.

"Rachel! Rachel!" Mr. Russell called.

"Coming, Dad!" she called up the stairs.

Andy watched his sister go into his parents' bedroom and close the door. He imagined his sister saying, "What if she snores? What then?" But then he realized Rachel liked Tamika as much as he did.

His parents' bedroom door opened and Mr. Russell said, "Andy, could you please come in here."

Andy walked slowly into their room. He looked at his mother. She was sitting on their bed, propped up with pillows. She was smiling.

"Andy," Mrs. Russell said, "your father, Rachel, and I have talked it over, and until Tamika's parents get better—or until the Perlmans return from South America—we would like to be her foster family."

"You would? Really?"

"And," Mr. Russell said, "Rachel said Tamika could stay in her room."

"Can I call her? Can I tell her?" Andy asked.

"Yes, you may," Mrs. Russell said. "And I'd like to speak with her, too."

Andy called Tamika from his parents' room. "They said *yes!*" Andy shouted into the telephone. "Oh, I'm sorry for screaming, Mrs. Perlman," he said softly. "This is Andy. Can I please speak with Tamika."

Hurry, please, hurry, Andy thought.

Andy waited.

Oh, what's taking you so long? Andy wondered.

"Tamika, Tamika!" Andy said when she finally got on the telephone. "I have some good news. No, the *best* news. The best news ever."

Andy told Tamika she could live with his family.

"Oh, this is so great!" Tamika cried. "I don't want to change schools. I don't want to live in someone's house who I don't even know. I'm so happy." Then she asked, "Are you sure your parents said I could live with you?" But she didn't wait for Andy to answer. "And the Perlmans were worried about what would happen to their house while they're away. Now I can watch it for them. I can water their plants and feed their fish. And we can do homework together every night! Oh, this is so great!"

"May I talk to her?" Andy's mother asked.

When Mrs. Russell took the telephone, Tamika told her, "Oh, thank you. Thank you so much."

"You don't have to thank me," Mrs. Russell said. "We haven't done anything yet, and I know it will be our pleasure to have you here. But there are a lot of arrangements to be made first. May I talk to Mrs. Perlman?"

Mrs. Russell and Mrs. Perlman talked about the foster agency. Mrs. Perlman said she would talk with the people at the agency and that Mr. Rutledge, Tamika's caseworker, would probably call to meet the Russells.

Ding! Ding!

The front doorbell rang.

Andy's mother was still talking to Mrs. Perlman on the phone. She waved to Andy, gesturing for him to see who was at the door.

Andy ran downstairs. He pushed open the mail slot, looked through it, and saw Tamika's knees. Andy quickly opened the door and they hugged.

"This is so great!" Tamika said. "But there's just one thing."

"I know," Andy told her. "The agency."

"No, not that. That's not a problem. Someone from the agency will come here to talk to your family. No, that's not it."

Andy waited.

Suddenly Tamika didn't seem so excited.

"What is it?" Andy asked.

Tamika took a small step back. She was looking down. "It's my parents," she said softly. "I want them to meet you and your family before we do anything, before I move in—even before we talk to the agency."

"Sure," Andy said.

"You see, I've told them about you, but just that you're my friend. If I'm going to live here, they have to meet you and your parents."

"Sure," Andy said again.

"Maybe we can go tomorrow, after school."

"Yeah, sure. I'll ask my parents."

Tamika waited by the door while Andy went upstairs.

Mrs. Russell was in bed. Her eyes were closed. Andy leaned real close to see if she was sleeping.

"Mom," Andy whispered.

She didn't respond.

Andy got even closer. Their noses almost touched. "Mom," he whispered again.

Mrs. Russell opened her eyes. "Oh my," she said. "What are you doing?"

"I was just seeing if you're sleeping," Andy said. "I have to ask you something."

"I *was* resting," Mrs. Russell said. "Now, what's your question?"

"Where's Dad? I have to ask him, too."

Mrs. Russell rubbed her eyes and said, "He's in the attic."

Andy went into the closet. The rope ladder was hanging down from the open hatchway in the ceiling.

"Dad," Andy called up toward the hatchway, "I have to ask you and Mom something."

Mr. Russell came to the hatchway and looked down at Andy. "What is it?"

Andy stood at the door to the closet. He looked from his mother, who was sitting up in her bed, to his father in the attic. "Tamika is real happy about living here, but before she moves in, her parents have to meet us. Can we go see them tomorrow?"

"I can be home by four tomorrow afternoon," Mr. Russell said. "We can go then."

"And we'll take Rachel," Mrs. Russell added.

Andy hurried downstairs to tell Tamika.

"That's good," she said, "and *please,* don't tell anyone at school about this until we're sure. Don't even tell Bruce."

The next day in school, Andy had to stop and think before he spoke. He could talk to Tamika about their secret, but not about his mom being pregnant. And he could talk to Bruce about that, but not about Tamika. This was a lot for Andy to keep track of. He was glad the gerbils were all back in their tanks and he didn't have to worry about keeping that secret anymore.

He paid attention in class and even answered a math problem correctly. When he did, Stacy Ann Jackson turned to face him and said, "Lucky guess." But Andy knew he wasn't just lucky. If only he could pay attention in class, he would be a good student. If only Ms. Roman wasn't so boring.

Tamika went to the Russells' house after school, and at four o'clock they all went to the rehabilitation center to visit with Tamika's parents.

It was a short drive to the center. Mr. Russell parked the car and everyone followed Tamika to the front entrance. They all signed the visitors' book and the man at the front desk gave them each a visitor's pass to clip on their shirts. Andy and his parents and Rachel followed Tamika into the elevator.

"This place smells funny," Andy whispered, but no one responded.

As they got off on the third floor, a nurse wheeled an old man into the elevator. The man's head was resting on his shoulder.

Tamika gently touched his hand and said, "Hello, Mr. Fischer."

He smiled.

While the nurse kept her foot by the elevator door to keep it from closing, she told Tamika, "Your parents are in the solarium."

"Thank you," Tamika said, and went to the left, leading the Russells down a long hallway lined with doors. The place was quiet and warm, and Andy felt uncomfortable there.

The first door they passed was open. Andy looked in and saw an old woman, with long white hair, sitting in a wheelchair and looking up at a television mounted on the wall. The woman was wearing a robe and slippers. Andy felt he shouldn't be looking at the woman in her robe, so he quickly turned away, and when they passed other open doors in the hall, Andy was careful not to look in.

The Russells followed Tamika to a room with large windows. People were sitting in front of a large television set. There was a game show on and the host was shouting about some prize, but most of the seated people didn't seem to be paying any attention to him. Tamika walked past them to two people who were sitting by one of the large windows, with their backs to the television.

Mr. Russell whispered, "They must be Tamika's parents."

The Russells stood quietly and waited until Tamika signaled for them to come over. Andy didn't know why his parents and Rachel walked forward so slowly, but he knew why he did: He was a little scared. He wondered what people looked like after a really bad car accident.

"You have to stand here," Tamika said, pointing directly in front of her parents. "It's hard for them to turn."

Andy walked to a spot in front of the two

wheelchairs. He was looking down, so the first he saw of the Andersons was their feet, resting on small square metal plates attached to each chair. Andy looked up a little and saw their hands. Their feet and hands looked fine to Andy, until he realized they didn't move. Then Andy looked up and saw their faces, bent slightly forward. They looked like regular people to Andy, regular people who stayed very still.

"Mom, Dad," Tamika said. "These are my friends, Andy and Rachel."

"Hello," Andy said. He started to step forward and reach out to shake Mr. Anderson's hand, but he quickly pulled his hand back.

Rachel smiled. She slowly lifted her right hand and waved it a little.

Mr. Anderson mumbled something.

"Dad said, 'Hello,' " Tamika explained.

"And these are Mr. and Mrs. Russell," Tamika said.

"You have a wonderful daughter," Mrs. Russell said. "You must be very proud of her."

Tamika's mom and dad smiled. Mr. Anderson mumbled something.

"My dad said, 'Thank you,' " Tamika explained.

"We hope Tamika can stay with us for a while," Mrs. Russell said. "She'll stay in Rachel's room. We have an extra bed there."

The Andersons smiled again. Andy assumed their smiles meant, "Yes, she *can* stay with you."

Mrs. Anderson said, "We think Tamika is the sweetest girl in the world and you have all been the nicest friends to her."

She spoke a lot more clearly than Mr. Anderson. Andy understood her easily.

"Tamika talks about you all the time," Mrs. Anderson continued. "She loves you all, and if she loves you, so do we."

Tamika blushed.

There were tears in Andy's eyes when Mrs. Anderson said Tamika loved him and his family.

Mrs. Russell patted Mrs. Anderson's hand. Mr. Russell just smiled.

Andy and his parents and Rachel stood there for another couple of minutes, until Mrs. Russell said, "Tamika, we'll wait for you by the elevator."

"You visit as long as you want," Mr. Russell

said, turning to walk away. "We don't mind waiting."

As Andy walked through the hall of the rehabilitation center, he thought about the escaped gerbils, Rachel's chewed-up autograph book, and his problems with Ms. Roman, and he realized those weren't *real* troubles. At least his parents were healthy and he didn't have to live in someone else's house.

When they were all downstairs, Tamika said in a determined voice that Andy hadn't heard before, "My parents look *very* good and they're getting better. It's just taking a long time."

Tamika stopped, turned to face Andy, and said, "It's so good I have friends like you, your family, and the Perlmans."

Tamika smiled and that made Andy feel better.

In the car everyone discussed having Tamika move in. They made all kinds of plans: where she would hang her clothes, where she and Andy would do their homework, how they would make her a real—though temporary—member of the family. Mrs. Russell asked her what she liked to eat for breakfast. Everyone seemed really happy.

Early the next week, Mr. Rutledge came from

the agency and looked at the room Tamika would share with Rachel. Then he sat by the kitchen table. Andy and Rachel waited in the living room while Mr. Rutledge spoke with Mr. and Mrs. Russell. Soon the Russells joined Andy in the living room and told Rachel to go talk with Mr. Rutledge in the kitchen.

"Did he have lots of questions?" Andy asked. "Is he nice? Did he say Tamika can live here?"

"Don't worry so much," Mr. Russell said.

But Andy *did* worry.

Rachel came out of the kitchen. She was smiling. "Your turn," she said to Andy.

Mr. Rutledge was writing in a large folder. Andy stood by the entrance to the kitchen and waited. Mr. Rutledge stopped writing. Then he turned and saw Andy standing there.

"Come in," Mr. Rutledge said. "Sit down."

Andy sat in his regular place at the table.

"So you're Andy Russell," Mr. Rutledge said, and smiled.

"Is that good?" Andy asked.

"Yes. Yes," Mr. Rutledge assured Andy. "It's very good. Tamika has told me some very nice things about you."

"Really?"

"Yes, really," Mr. Rutledge answered.

"Now," Mr. Rutledge continued, "are you aware that Tamika would not simply be coming for a visit? She would be living here."

"Yes," Andy answered. "That would be *so* great."

"When Tamika is here," Mr. Rutledge went on, "you would have two sisters, not just one."

Andy smiled.

Then Mr. Rutledge asked, "Do you and Rachel get along?"

Andy looked down at the table and said softly, "Sometimes we argue."

"Do you hit each other?" Mr. Rutledge asked.

"No," Andy said. "We just argue."

Mr. Rutledge smiled. "All siblings argue," he said. "That's normal."

Mr. Rutledge wrote in his folder. He looked up for a moment and Andy expected him to say something. But he just smiled to himself, looked down again, and wrote some more.

Andy didn't know what to do. He felt uncomfortable watching Mr. Rutledge write, but he didn't think he should just leave the kitchen.

Maybe, he thought, *he has something else to ask me.*

Andy sat there for a while, but there were no more questions. Then Mr. Rutledge closed the folder and called Andy's parents and Rachel into the kitchen.

"Of course," he told them, "I will recommend that your home be approved by the agency. And I'm sure Tamika will be very happy here."

The Russells thanked him and walked with him to the door.

Andy waited for the door to close. He looked through the mail slot and watched Mr. Rutledge get into his car. Then, when he was sure Mr. Rutledge could not hear him, Andy stretched out his arms and shouted, "YAHOO!" He hugged his parents. He even hugged Rachel.

"This is good news," Mr. Russell said.

"But it won't be easy for Tamika," Mrs. Russell cautioned. "We have to make her feel comfortable here, that we're her family."

Andy wasn't worried about that.

That night, before Andy fell asleep, he thought about the future. Tamika would be living in his house and that would be great. He thought about the school carnival. That would be fun. And if he gave away all of his gerbils, maybe he could get some other animals to put in the tanks—maybe chameleons or a gecko. Then Andy thought about his mother and the new baby. *It wouldn't be so bad if it turned out to be a girl. Maybe the girl will grow up to be like Tamika. That would be OK. Or maybe it will be a boy, a boy like me. That would be OK, too.*

Turn the page for a sneak peek at Andy's next adventure. . . .

Now all of Andy's secrets are safely out and all the problems are safely solved. So his troubles are over, right?

Wrong!

In *Andy and Tamika,* Andy and the gerbils get into more trouble, this time at school. With the school carnival coming up and the Perlmans leaving, Andy has enough worries without teacher's pet Stacy Ann Jackson nosing into his business. And what about the baby? Will it be a boy or a girl, and what should its name be? Andy's not the only one dying to find out!